Loved Alone

Molly Likovich

Also by Molly Likovich

Sexy Sleepy Hollow Series

Send in The Clowns

There's Something in The Woods

Be Terrible

Falling for Jack Frost

The Firefighter Before Christmas

Not a Myth

The Willow's Silence

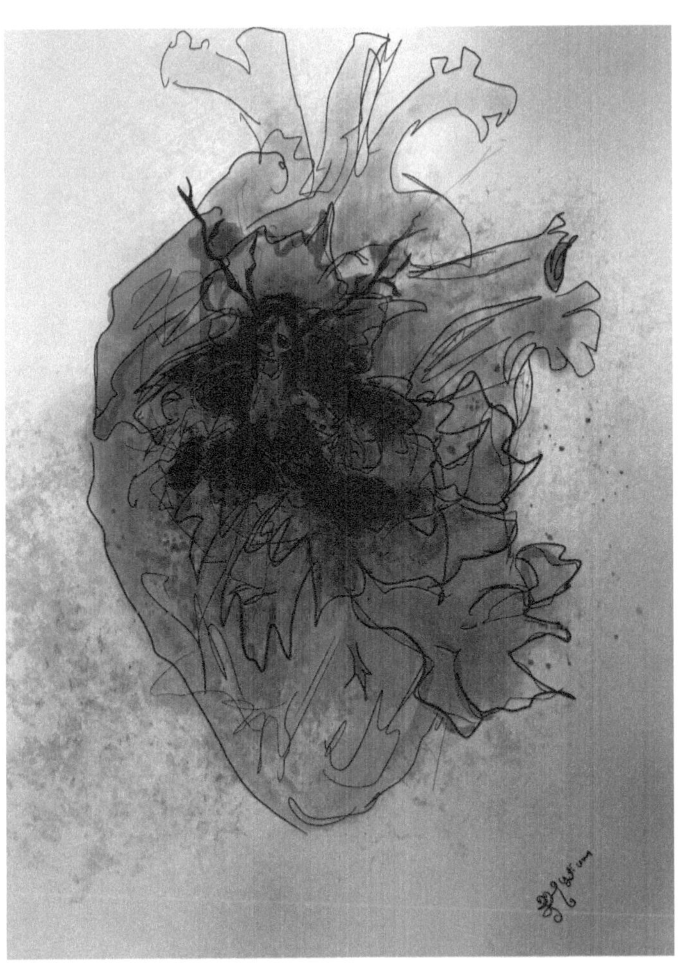

*"Everything we see or seem is but a dream within a
dream."*

— Edgar Allan Poe

Content Warning

This novel is inspired by the life and works of Edgar
Allan Poe,
it is not a biographical account; some aspects have been
added, exaggerated, or imagined. This story also deals with
topics of mental illness, substance abuse, and suicide. Please
proceed with caution.

Chapter 1

*She was a child and I was a child,
in this kingdom by the sea*

Richmond Virginia, 1826

Annabel walked out of the ocean like a mermaid—a siren coming to lure him out to sea.

"What's wrong?" She asked as she came to stand before him, her white dress thoroughly soaked. He could see her skin—pale like the moon eternally above them —through the thin fabric. He knew it was wrong to look, but he was young and wild with want for her.

"I think…" his mind wandered.

He knew there was somewhere else. Somewhere else he was coming from, but sometimes it was hazy here on this beach with Annabel's eyes gazing into his.

"My father," he said finally, beginning to get his thoughts in order. "It's about my father."

"What's he done this time?" Annabel asked.

"He won't send me…"

"Send you what?"

"Money for soap and clothes."

Annabel frowned.

"Where are you, Edgar? You're not here."

He was never there. They weren't anywhere. They were nowhere.

"Annabel," he whispered, pressing his icy hand against her cheek. "Are you real? Or are you all in my head?"

She smiled and placed her hand on top of his.

"Dearest, Edgar," she murmured against the crash of the waves. "I'm both."

* * *

"Edgar, you need to wake up now."

Edgar startled awake, lifting his head off of the bar. He looked across the way to see Mary frowning at him. She had sweat glistening on her brow, and the scent of whisky and wine wafted off her like perfume.

"I think you've had enough, Eddie."

Edgar frowned right back, but he knew she was right.

"What's my bill?" He asked, wiping rum-slick sweat from his own brow.

"You know I don't charge you, Eddie."

"You should."

"You can't pay."

He felt himself swell with shame.

"I know."

"It's alright," she said, patting his hand. "One day you'll be able to. You'll sell loads of stories and poems and be rich and famous. Like all the greats. Then you can take me out for a feast."

"I wish I believed your words, Mary."

"Me too," she said, taking the rag from her shoulder and began to wipe down the bar. "You're one of the greats in the making, trust me. Have I ever been wrong?"

Edgar reached for his glass, only to realize she'd moved it.

Mary had never been wrong.

"Don't you have class in the morning?" She asked.

He nodded.

"Are you going to go?"

He shrugged.

Mary looked around the empty tavern, then hoisted herself up onto the bar. She swung her legs around so that they dangled on either side of Edgar. Her skirt was hitched up from the motion and her cheeks were rosy with obvious desire. Edgar always knew he should discourage this, and he never did.

"Tell me a story, Eddie."

He smiled.

"On a stormy night, a man sits alone in his study when he hears a rapping at his window..."

* * *

"What do you want?" Mrs. Royster asked when she opened the door.

Edgar wrung his hands together, digging his nails into the flesh of his palms.

"I'm here to see Elmira."

"She's not here."

"Oh..."

Mrs. Royster glared at him.

"Didn't your father tell you?"

"Tell me what, ma'am?"

If eyes could set another aflame, Edgar would be ablaze with this woman's hatred for him.

"Elmira's married."

* * *

"What have you done?" Edgar shouted as he stormed into John Allan's study.

John Allan looked up from his ledger with nothing but distaste for his foster son evident in his eyes.

"What are you shouting about?"

"Elmira!"

"I'm busy, Edgar. Go bother someone else. I think Stanley is around somewhere."

John Allan waved his hand in the air, as if he was talking about a dog and not one of the people he kept as property. Edgar seethed.

"She's married!"

John Allan looked back up from his ledger.

"I am aware that Sarah Royster is married. She is now Mrs. Alexander Shelton. I was at the wedding, it was a charming service."

"How could you do this to me?" Edgar begged with tears in his eyes.

John Allan sighed in annoyance.

"I fail to see how Sarah marrying has anything to do with either of us."

"She was my fiance!"

John Allan laughed as tears began to stream down Edgar's face.

"Don't be delusional."

"Mrs. Royster told me, she told me you fixed the whole thing."

John Allan was silent.

Edgar shook his head.

"Why do you hate me so ardently?" He whispered. "What have I ever done to deserve such abuse?"

John Allan stood up, slamming his hands down on his desk as he did.

"I feed you, I house and clothe you. Please explain to me how you've suffered abuse? My lord, Edgar, you behave as if I treat you like the slaves. Do I make you work in the fields? No. I pay for your education. I pay for—"

"You ignore my letters! I'm practically starving and you don't even care!"

"It is not my fault that you are unable to adhere to the budget I provide for you."

Edgar felt his face grow warm as his anxiety and despair bloomed in his chest.

"I love her," he said helplessly. "And she loves me."

John Allan sat back down, returning his attention to his ledger.

"Did you hear me?" Edgar demanded, taking a step closer to the desk. "I love her and she loves me."

"Clearly not."

Those two words stuck Edgar; a bullet to the heart. He was bleeding out right there on the floor and his father paid him no mind.

"How can you do this to me?" He begged once more. "I'm your son."

"No," John Allan said, "you're not."

* * *

"Annabel!" Edgar called out as a violent storm consumed the sea. "Annabel, where are you?"

"Edgar?"

Edgar turned to see Annabel standing amidst the waves, her hair soaked from the rain. He rushed into the water, shedding his jacket so it wouldn't weigh him down. When he finally reached her, she was shivering. She smelled like salt and death. His teeth chattered and heart ached.

"It never storms here," she whispered. "What's happening?"

Edgar tilted his head back and looked up at the sky.

"Where are you, Edgar, when you're not here?"

He looked back into her forget-me-not blue eyes and saw his own sorrow reflected back in them.

"I see things," he whispered against the storm. "When I'm not here. I see you."

"I'm always here, Edgar."

Edgar felt tears in his eyes.

"Annabel, have we met before? Before coming here?"

"Edgar," her voice was soft, her eyes were dry

"There was never anything for us before here."

Chapter 2

Music of the passion-hearted

Boston Massachusetts, 1829

The pub was loud, Edgar wished the world would quiet down just for a bit. Just so he could get his thoughts straight.

"Eddie!" Petronella came rushing into the pub, flinging her arms around Edgar and kissing the top of his head.

She sat down opposite him and placed a book on the table between them.

Al Aaraaf, Tamerlane & Minor Poems

"You bought it," he said, smiling.

He gently touched the cover, worried it might be a specter that would vanish into the night at any moment.

"Of course I bought it! I read it already. It's wonderful."

He looked up and into Petronella's deep, brown eyes. Her dark skin looked beautiful in the candlelight, he imagined she would look even more beautiful with the moon strung up behind her. Or the sun shining down brightly on her face. He wished they could see each other outside of the walls of this dim and dusty hole-in-the-wall.

"You really liked it?" He asked.

"Of course I did. It's brilliant. *"Fair flowers, and fairy! To whose care is given to bear the Goddess song, in odors up to heaven."*

Edgar laughed softly in disbelief.

"You've memorized lines?"

"One day I'll memorize them all. One day the world will, too, Edgar."

He thought back to Mary's legs swinging over the bar of the tavern back in Virginia. He missed her. He often longed for Petronella in similar ways but he could never seem to tell if she felt the same way for him. Surely memorizing his verses was confirmation that she did?

Several hours passed and the two made their way through many glasses of whisky and wine until the world wasn't quite so loud. The shadows that had been following him all night finally slipped away into the corners and eventually out the door. His mind was just a bit closer to peace.

"Let me walk you home, Nella."

Edgar gazes into her eyes, a look of pure surprise painted in them.

"Eddie, no."

"I won't ask to come up."

"Eddie...what if someone were to see us?"

He reached across and took her hand in his.

"Let them."

And so they donned their coats and headed out into the chilly, night air. Edgar wanted to wrap Petronella up in his arms but he knew that couldn't be done out in the open.

When they finally reached her boarding house he was ravenous with his hunger for her.

"I lied," he said softly.

Petronella looked at him again, this time with a weariness he couldn't quite make sense of.

"Let me come up, Nella."

"Eddie," she said softly.

"No one's around to see. I wouldn't let—"

"It's not that," she said softly.

He took a step away from her. "Forgive me. You were just being kind and I misread it."

Petronella looked at him still, her weariness turning to sadness.

"You misunderstand me.."

"Then help me understand."

"You're a poet."

"That I am," he said, somewhat proudly.

Petronella took a breath that shook like shutters in a storm.

"You may forget," she said, "but let me tell you this: someone in some future time will think of us."

In his drunken state it took him a moment longer than it should have to realize who she was quoting.

Sappho.

"Oh."

Petronella was trying not to cry.

"Do you hate me now?" She whispered.

"What? Nella, no. Gods no. You're my—" he stepped closer to her, taking her in his arms and holding her. He tilted his head down just so. He looked into her eyes, truly seeing her for the first time. All of her. "You're my best friend. I could never hate you."

"There are those who...well you know, you were raised Christian."

"Yes," he said. "Christians who thought it was right and just to own people. Whatever their God's words say is right and wrong is no concern of mine."

Pretonella wiped at her tears.

"You don't think it's a sin?"

He shook his head and pulled her close. She wrapped her arms around his back and he rested his chin on her head, breathing in the sweet, floral scent of her hair.

"Loving isn't a sin."

* * *

Edgar awoke in a starry garden. He sat up and looked around in confusion. He was wearing only his nightshirt. He got up on shaky legs but his head was no longer sluggish from drink. He felt slightly panicked upon realizing this. He wasn't ready to see the shadows again. To hear their screams.

"Hello," said a soft, melodic voice.

Edgar turned around to see a great, glorious tree and standing beneath it, wearing a dress woven from glimmering leaves, a beautiful woman.

"Hello," he said. "Where am I?"

She tilted her head to the side.

"Don't you know?"

Edgar shook his head. "I'm afraid not."

"Who are you?"

"Edgar. Edgar Allan Poe."

The beautiful woman smiled. "Hello Edgar, I'm Nesace."

Edgar felt his heart go still for a moment.

"But…"

Nesace began to walk towards him.

"Don't you know me? *Twas a sweet time for Nesace—for there her world lay lolling on a*

golden air."

She came to stand before him. She looked so much like Petronella and also nothing like her at all. She had Petronella's eyes, but her hair was a rich red—like mulled wine. And her skin was several shades darker. She was taller, too. Nearly as tall as Edgar.

"You read my poem?"

"I am your poem, aren't I?"

"No," he said, shaking his head. "It's just a story. It's not real. You're not real."

"Since when are stories not real?"

"I don't…" he shook his head again. Was this better or worse than the shadows? "Am I asleep?"

"You're wide awake," she said. "Here with us."

"Us?"

"The others are waiting. Come along."

Nesace took his hand in hers and began to lead him further into the star-soaked garden. Eventually they reached a long, ivory table that had lilies woven all throughout it. Sitting at the table were three new faces. Beautiful faces. Edgar was nearly struck dumb by them.

"Edgar," said a woman in white. "We're so glad you're here. I'm Ianthe."

Edgar felt breathless. He felt light as air. He slowly spun around, allowing himself to fully take in the beauty of the magnificent garden, and the way the sky above them seemed to drip with starlight. He looked back at the table full of beauty. He smiled. He spoke:

"A sound of silence on the startled ear which dreamy

poets name 'the music of the sphere.' Ours is a world of worlds."

The four faces smiled back to him.

* * *

"Tell me about her."

Edgar looked over at Petronella. They were sitting on her roof, early winter snow falling down and dusting them like sugar.

"Who?"

"The girl you dream about. I see her."

"Where?" He asked, startled.

"Your eyes. Your heart."

He frowned. He could tell her about Mary. It would be easier to speak about Mary's swinging legs and whisky-smile. Her cheeks blushed from the warm tavern and her eyes hazy from exhaustion. He could talk about how she asked him for stories and never made him pay his tab. He could talk about how his fingers twitched every time she was near; desperately wanting to touch her.

But that was not who Petronella was talking about.

"Her name is Elmira."

Petronella smiled. Warm as sunlight.

"That's a pretty name."

"It really is. Her first name is Sarah, but she didn't like it. No one would call her Elmira no matter how much she asked them to."

"Except you."

"Except me."

"What happened? Where did she go?"

Edgar frowned and kept his eyes on the stars.

Petronella knew him well.

She saw the truth.

She reached out and took his hand in hers. He didn't look away from the stars and she didn't ask him to. They sat in the silence that only perfect soul mates can. It didn't matter that she couldn't fall in love with him, she loved him better than anyone ever had.

* * *

The shadows were back. Edgar was trying to write on a dreary night, tucked up in the tiny, drafty room he rented, when he saw them; lurking in the corners of the room. Suddenly the air tasted rotten, and his clothes scratched at his skin; suffocating him. He jumped up from his

small desk and moved as far away from the shadows as he could manage. "What do you want?"

He whispered.

As a rule he tried to avoid ever addressing them. Because that meant he had to question if they were really real or not, and he didn't know which answer frightened him more.

Poeeeeee

"Are you a ghost?"

Silence.

The shadow began to flicker like dark candlelight.

"Are you a demon?"

The shadow seemed to take shape and then it unhinged its jaw and screamed.

Edgar collapsed to the floor, hands pressed firmly over his ears as his breathing became ragged and he did his best to block it out.

"Not real. Not real. Not real."

He looked back up, the shadow was silent but still there.

He crawled across the room, back to his desk, and pulled open the small, bottom drawer. He took out a bottle of whisky, opened it, and threw back the biggest gulp he could manage. Twenty minutes later he was lying flat on his back in blissful silence. There were no screaming shadows. There was only the peace of a quiet mind.

* * *

Petronella fell ill the following summer. Edgar knew this narrative too well. He wanted to sit by her bedside but he knew that role fell to her lover; a woman he had never even met. Edgar went to the pub alone, sipping wine alone, re-reading his own little book wondering what other lines Petronella liked best.

Autumn was nearly there when a raven-haired woman with an emerald-green bonnet found her way to his table hidden away in the farthest corner of the pub. Edgar realized who she was before she had even taken her seat.

"Are you Mr. Allan Poe?"

"Call me Edgar."

The woman nodded.

"I'm Petronella's friend."

Edgar nodded.

"I know," he said, his words beginning to slur slightly. The large bottle of port before him was almost empty.

"I see," she said. "My name's Annie."

"Nice to meet you, Annie. Are you here because..."

Annie nodded.

"She's gone. She went last night in her sleep."

"Oh," Edgar said, his voice sounded hollow and empty to his own ears. "What was..."

"Consumption."

"Oh. I see."

"I know you loved her," Annie said.

Edgar reached for the bottle of port.

"She was my best friend."

Annie nodded. "Mine too. This is for you."

Annie slid a letter across the small table to Edgar, then got up and left without another word.

He looked down at the letter, forlornly. His name was written on it in simple script: *Eddie.* He sighed softly and opened it, pulling out the parchment inside.

Eddie, if you're reading this then the end has come. I will miss you. But please don't let sadness get the best of you. Go forth and be remarkable. Show the rest of the world what a talent you are. Be the great writer I know you are.

He got up, crumpled the note in his hand, and tossed it into the fire.

Chapter 3

Events which had taken place in sober

Baltimore Maryland, 1831

Dear Mary,

I am writing to you from Baltimore. My aunt reached out to me, offering to let me come live with her and my cousin Virginia. I was running low on funds—Al Aaraaf didn't sell quite as many copies as I had hoped—so I took her up on the offer.

It is strange here. Not the best. The air is hot and stifling in this small house, and the walls are as thin as flimsy promises. Every sigh can be heard from every corner.

My aunt is also like my father in many ways. She does not hold the progressive views of many here in the North when it comes to the way humans ought to be treated.

I wish you were here, Mary. I could use a friendly face. I await your reply with anxiety, I am often a wreck as I anticipate the delivery of the post. I'm sure you have some clever way to mock me for such a trait, please include such a mockery in your reply.

Yours truly,
Edgar

* * *

"**E**dgar!"

Edgar sighed as he looked up from his letter at the sound of his aunt Maria's screeching voice. He came down the narrow flight of steps from his tiny attic room, and made his way to the top of the main staircase of the house. It was more of an alcove with steps, the house was too compact to have anything more.

"Yes, Aunt?"

"There's someone here to see you."

No one ever came to see Edgar. His only friends were Mary who was still back in his hometown, and his cousin Virginia and she was only a young girl. But his aunt didn't seem to care much about why her nephew looked so perplexed and retreated back to the kitchen to finish her chores for the day.

Edgar slowly and somewhat nervously made his way down the alcove and through the back to the sitting room at the front of the house.

Standing just inside the doorway was a young man that Edgar recognized. His jaw dropped as he looked into the eyes of a soul he had not seen in decades. A soul he thought he would never be blessed enough to see again.

"Henry?" Edgar whispered.

The man smiled broadly—joyously.

"Hello, brother."

Edgar broke out into a smile of his own, tears of joy in his eyes as he threw himself across the room and into his brother's arms.

* * *

Edgar and Henry went out drinking. The night came upon them quickly, the stars dimmed by the drink on their tongues. The two laughed and cheered and it was as if no time had ever passed. Once Edgar was thoroughly drunk his mind began to wander. It was as if he and Henry were children again. But the childhood he began to see dance across his memory wasn't the one he had lived. This one was different. Better. Brighter.

He smiled to himself as false dreams of growing up with his brother by his side filled his mind. But soon the dreams of a happier life melted away like candle wax. His real memories washed in and the horrors of his adoptive father's abuse crowded his mind.

The walls of the pub began to move and the floor began to tilt. Without thinking Edgar got up and rushed from the building, his body no longer his own. He heard his brother calling out to him but the shadows were beginning to take form outside of his mind.

"No, no, no, no," he whispered as he raced down the sidewalk.

He was drunk. The drink was supposed to banish the

shadows. He didn't know how he would ever bear having to see them even when he was soaked with wine.

"Edgar!" Henry called out.

But when Edgar turned to look back at his brother all he could see was the shadow behind him. It wasn't Henry's shadow, it was a looming, horrible, monster that Edgar knew had come to destroy him. He knew it came to drive him mad. To end him in every way imaginable. The shadow opened its mouth and began to speak. It spoke with John Allan's voice and Edgar crashed to his knees, sobbing.

"Edgar!" Henry said again, rushing to his brother and taking him in his arms.

Edgar rocked back and forth against the warmth of Henry's body and continued to sob as the shadow's speaking changed to shouting. Edgar covered his ears and begged with the dark specter to free him from this torment, but it was unrelenting.

"What's wrong, brother?" Henry kept asking but Edgar had no words, and even if he did, how could he ever explain such madness to his brother in a way that would make any sense?

The shadow screeched like a wild animal and then there was only darkness.

* * *

Edgar awoke to the sight of a gray-eyed man gazing down at him.

"Where am—"

"Shhh," the man said, tersely. "We must be quiet now."

The man reached out his hand and Edgar took it. As the gray-eyed man helped him up to sitting, Edgar realized he had been laying on a grand, dining table. He looked around and saw that he was in a vast and sprawling manor; one even more lavish than John Allan's. Edgar looked back at the stern man with the stormy eyes. The man held a candlestick whose light reflected a look of sorrow in his stare.

"Do I know you?" Edgar whispered, heeding the man's prior admonishment.

"Not yet."

The man began to walk away, waving his hand for Edgar to follow.

Together they traveled in silence down many winding, marble halls; the only sound was the flicker of the candle flame and the soft padding of their feet.

"My sister," the man began, "is dead. She died last night."

"I'm terribly sorry," Edgar said.

They walked on in silence.

"I...I had a sister as well."

The man stopped and looked at Edgar.

"Do you miss her terribly?"

Edgar nodded. "With every bone in my body."

"What else have you lost?"

Elmira.

"Too much," Edgar breathed.

The man nodded.

"Follow me."

Edgar did and the gray-eyed man led them into a study. He sat Edgar down in an armchair and poured them each a glass of brandy. There was already a fire burning in the hearth; the two men sat staring into the flames and sipping their spirits in silence.

"Who are you?" Edgar asked.

"Roderick Usher. My sister Madeline Usher is dead."

"You keep saying that."

Roderick looked over at Edgar.

"Because it is true."

"Then why," Edgar said, setting his drink down on the end table, the glass shaking from the sound, "can I hear her screaming?"

The glass shattered with the pitch of Madeline's scream. Roderick jumped up, his eyes wide with horror. The screams got louder and louder and soon a Madeline-shaped shadow began to float up from the fire.

Edgar jumped up, moving back, practically falling over the chair.

"I've...good God," Roderick breathed. He grabbed Edgar's arm. "I've buried her alive!"

The screams became deafening.

Madeline's buried voice soon was drowned out by the sound of crashing waves.

Edgar! Edgar, come back to me!

Edgar looked to the door of the study.

Annabel was standing there, her white dress billowing out around her, the ocean at her back. She held her hand out to him.

"I'm sorry," Edgar whispered to Roderick.

He turned and ran.

He crashed into Annabel's arms and together they fell back into the sea.

Salt water filled his lungs and sank into his bones as he held onto Annabel as tight as he could. The door slammed shut and sunk into the ocean, never to be seen again.

The couple broke the surface of the fierce water, drinking in gulps of air.

Edgar wrapped an arm around Annabel's waist and helped guide them to shore. Together they crawled onto the wet sand, collapsing onto their backs, coughing up bits of the sea.

Edgar reached out for Annabel's hand and brought it to his lips. He gently kissed her knuckles and then let her hand rest over his heart.

"Edgar," she whispered.

He squeezed her hand and looked into her beautiful, bright eyes.

"I was scared," he confessed. "Terrified. I become more and more frightened with every passing day. Annabel, I fear I'm going mad."

"So what if you are?"

"What?"

She shifted closer to him in the sand, pressing her body against his as the water tickled their toes, trying to lure them back out to sea.

"Even if you are mad, entirely insane, what does it matter? In the end you're still you. You're still brilliant and passionate. You're still so full of love and ambition. You're still you, Edgar."

"But what if..." his voice vanished into the air as tears he was ashamed to shed began to well up in his eyes.

Annabel shifted closer again, held her hand to his cheek, and pressed her mouth to his. She tasted of salt and lemon. If peace and dreams had a flavor it was Annabel Lee.

"I love you, Edgar Allan Poe. Madman or not. You will always be the one my heart belongs to."

Edgar looked deep into her ocean-bright eyes, dazzling him like stars, then kissed her again—fiercer this time. He tangled his hands in her sea-soaked hair, opening his mouth wider to invite her in. She obeyed, offering her tongue and teeth up to him. He dragged her on top of him and caressed her back through the thin, soaked fabric of her dress.

Annabel writhed against him, her breath coming out in gasps and soft moans. Edgar began to move with her, their clothes creating a damp friction between them.

"My heart is yours, Annabel. My soul is yours. I'm yours."

"Forever?" She whispered.

"*Forever.*"

Annabel propped herself up just enough to look down at him. She smiled and it was the most beautiful thing he had ever seen. He knew he must find a way to one day commit her beauty—her *radiance*—to words.

"Time to wake up now, my love," she whispered.

"Annabel, no, don't leave me. Please, not yet."

* * *

"Edgar!"

Edgar opened his eyes. Henry was looking down at him, relief filled his eyes upon seeing Edgar awaken.

"Oh thank the Lord!"

Henry pulled Edgar into his arms from where he was sprawled across the sidewalk. A small group of late night drinkers and workers had gathered around to either find entertainment in the breakdown of a madman, or to worry about his condition.

"Are you alright, Edgar?" Henry asked.

Edgar wanted to scream. He wanted to be back on that beach with Annabel where things made sense. Where his heart was at peace. Where he was finally able to feel happiness.

But this was his brother. His brother who had been lost to him for years. If Annabel told him it was time to go back to this waking world then he needed to trust her.

She's not even real.

Edgar pushed the thought away. Annabel had to be real. Usher, Madeline, and the deities of Al Aaraaf could all be figments of his wild and dark imagination, but Annabel needed to be real.

Elmira.

Edgar pushed that thought away. Elmira was lost to him long ago. Just like his sanity.

"Let's get you home," Henry said.

Edgar nodded and allowed his brother to help him to his feet.

Later as dawn was breaking Henry tucked Edgar into his tiny bed as if he were a child.

"I'm sorry, Henry."

"You have nothing to apologize for."

"I never wanted you to see me like this," Edgar said.

"Like what?" Henry asked. "Everyone falls ill, it's nothing to be embarrassed about."

"Henry," Edgar whispered, "this is no ordinary sickness."

There was a moment of silence between the two.

Edgar feared that this was it.

Henry would leave and he would never see his brother again.

He missed Mary.

He missed Petronella.

He missed Elmira and his birth parents he never got to know. He missed their sister. He missed the life he might have had if fortune had smiled on him just once.

"Well," Henry finally said, "ordinary is rather boring if you ask me."

* * *

A few months later Edgar stood between his cousin and aunt in the unforgiving summer heat and watched as his brother's body was lowered into the ground. Edgar had found him with a bottle in the end.

He wondered if his brother saw the same shadows.

Virginia reached out and took his hand in hers.

* * *

The witching hour was in full swing. Edgar was scribbling away, the stories beginning to take shape in his mind, and serving as a proper distraction from his grief.

"Edgar?"

He tore his eyes away from his quill and inkwell for the first time in hours.

Virginia stood at the top of the stairs to his room. A candlestick in her hand.

"What are you doing up, Virginia?"

"I heard you crying."

Edgar hesitated, then wiped at his face. Sure enough his fingers came away wet.

"I'm sorry," he said. "I did not realize."

"You're allowed to be sad," she said, coming over and sitting on his bed. "He was your brother."

Edgar took the candle from her and blew it out so she didn't accidentally set the bed aflame.

"Virginia, it's late. You should be in bed."

"I'm not a child, Edgar."

He smiled at his cousin.

"You're eight."

Virginia flopped back on his bed and he laughed.

"You have a nice laugh, cousin."

Edgar couldn't help but smile.

"And," she said, swinging back up and dangling her legs off the side of the bed, "I should like it if we could also be friends."

"I don't think your mother wants you to have friends like me."

"Why? Because you're poor and a drunk?"

There was a pause and then Edgar laughed.

"You're very forward, Virginia."

Virginia shrugged and flopped back on his bed with a smile.

"I get lonely, Edgar, and I know you do too, so let's be friends."

"Alright."

She shot up yet again.

"Really?" She asked, excitedly.

Edgar chuckled. "Yes, really."

She held her pinky finger out to him.

"Promise we'll always be friends."

Edgar leaned forward and linked his pinky with hers.

"I promise."

Chapter 4

Evil is a consequence of good, so, in fact out of joy is sorrow born

Baltimore Maryland, 1835

Edgar came home late, having been out drinking again. He didn't want to wake his aunt and cousin; they were finally starting to settle into a pattern of peace and he knew walking into the house in the middle of the night, loud and slovenly with drink, would cause that peace to shatter. So he crept up to his room as quietly as he could only to find Virginia sitting on his bed, reading an old copy of a magazine he had been published in.

"What piece were you reading?" He asked as he came to sit beside her.

"*Berenice.*"

"Virginia!"

"What?"

"You can't read stories like that!"

"All of your stories are like that."

"I am aware, cousin! They're not meant for young girls."

"I'm not a 'young girl' I'm almost thirteen."

"Thirteen is young, Virginia."

"Not young enough," she grumbled, getting up from the bed and heading for the stairs.

"What do you mean?" He asked after her.

Virginia went still at the top of the stairs, one of her hands braced against the wall.

"I'm not supposed to tell you," she said.

"But you will."

Virginia turned back around, her eyes locking on his.

"It's our cousin. Nielsen."

"What of him?"

"He's written to Mother, offering to take me away and educate me."

Edgar felt a tightness in his chest.

"Where would this education take place?"

"In his house."

"Virginia," Edgar said, fear creeping into his voice.

"Mother she...she doesn't think you're well, cousin. She said she would like me around more suitable company"

"I don't understand, why is Maria doing this? Why has Neilson made this offer?"

"They both seem to think that you wish to marry me."

"You're my cousin!"

Virginia sighed with the tone of annoyance that only girls of her age can master.

"People marry their cousins, Edgar. This is Maryland."

"I'm twice your age."

"Men older than you have married girls younger than me."

"That's ungodly."

"I agree. But unfortunately you and I do not make the rules of the world we live in." She stepped close to him and took one of his hands in her own. "Why do you think so many people like to get lost in the words you write? You give people a chance to experience something more fantastical than they could ever imagine. You craft stories of love and adventure that the rest of us will never get to know. You create legends with that quill. It's one of the many things I love about you. I couldn't ask for a better cousin. A better *friend*."

Edgar felt his shameful tears begin to betray him again. Oh, how he wished he could be made of stone and ice like so many other men his age. He closed his eyes to try and prevent them from falling.

"It's okay to cry," Virginia said gently.

Her words were warm against his skin. Soft, and comforting.

She squeezed his hand to let him know that she was still there.

"It is okay to *feel*. Do not let this awful world convince you any different."

He opened his eyes and looked down at his cousin. He saw how wise she was, but how young she was too. He was sickened by the idea of an old man taking her to bed and treating her like a grown woman. She was a girl and should be allowed to live as one; with innocence.

He thought of Elmira. They were both children when they professed their love for each other. A love he still felt, down to the very marrow of her bones. He never met her husband, he hoped the man was kind to her and not so old as to be cruel.

Virginia was his friend, his family, the only person who seemed to truly understand him. Petronella was gone. Henry was gone. Elmira was gone. He couldn't lose her too.'

"I don't want you to go," he said.

"I don't want to go either. But this is life, Edgar. People like us rarely get what we want."

* * *

"Do you believe in God, Anabel?"

Anabel lined up seashells in the shape of a star as Edgar approached her from the sea.

"No," she said. "Maybe."

"You're not sure?" He asked as he sat down beside her in the sand.

She continued to push seashells into place, creating different shapes in the sand, trying to tell a story through simple shapes.

"How can I be," she looked from her shapes and stars and into his eyes, "when I don't even know what I am?"

* * *

"You begged Mother for me to stay and now you're the one who's leaving?"

Maria stood at the top of the steps to the tiny Baltimore house, glaring down at her cousin as he loaded his suitcase into the back of the carriage.

"I'm sorry, Virginia, truly. But I've been given a job, at The Southern Literary Messenger no less."

"She will send me away now," Virginia said, a sorrow that was usually so foreign to her voice, seeping in. "They say it's to educate me but educating girls doesn't mean the same as it does for boys. I highly doubt I'm being sent off to read the works of Shakespeare, or to learn Latin or about the rules of government. No, I'll be sent to learn French, and which dinner spoon to use."

Edgar walked up a step so that he and Virginia were at eye level. He looked into her eyes and promised himself to keep her visage burned into his memory.

"French is a beautiful language, Sissy."

She groaned dramatically.

"Don't call me that, *Eddie*."

He smirked.

"Don't call me that," he mimicked back.

He had never told Virginia the real reason he didn't want to hear that nickname anymore.

"Do you really see me as your sister?"

"I see you as my friend. That's what you wanted, isn't it?"

She smiled and nodded.

"Then have a little faith that our friendship can withstand a bit of distance."

"Virginia is days away from Maryland."

"Write to me," he said.

"Write about me."

"I will."

Chapter 5

I must perish in this deplorable folly. Thus, thus, and not otherwise, shall I be lost

Richmond Virginia, 1836

Dear cousin,

I am sorry to be so brief and to ignore all the updates and poetry you included in your last correspondence but I fear that what I have to share with you is far too urgent and must take precedence over all of that. I do hope you can forgive my rudeness in this matter.

The urgency at hand is this: our cousin Nielson grows more and more persistent about my coming to live with him with each day that passes. He and Mother are convinced it is because of the love you have for me, they think that we are more than friends and both wish to supposedly save me from marrying at such a young age. Surely, cousin, you see this for the falsehood it is. They do not want me to marry a poor man. Nielson is rich. He is also a snake and I do not trust him and have no desire to be trapped in his home. There are rumors about him, about what kind of man he is; I do not think money equates goodness.

Please help me. You have said it yourself, I am young. Girls of my age are not meant to be anything other than silent, a wife, or both. You know me, cousin, I long to be neither.

Your Friend

* * *

Dear Sissy

I will help you any way that I can to save you from our cousin's house. I know better than most that many places are prisons hiding in plain sight. I will send money, as much as I can. Perhaps enough for you to make your way here. You could stay with me in the house I have here. It is small, but big enough to accommodate two reasonably well. Once you arrive we can figure out what to do moving forward.

Just tell me what you need and I shall give it, gladly.

Yours,
Edgar

* * *

Edgar,

Mother and Nielson will not take no for an answer. If I run away to Virginia Nielson will just hunt me down. And if not him there will always be other rich men in want of a young girl to be kept by their side—imprisoned in their home.

As a cousin you have no legal way to protect me. Women cannot belong to themselves in this world; we are bound to either our fathers or our husbands. I have neither.

Write to Mother and ask for my hand. They already think that we wish to marry so let us play into their delusion. Beg for me, Mother loves you deep down. She will give in if you plead a passionate enough case.

I anxiously await your reply.

Virginia

* * *

"I haven't seen you in years and the first thing you do is come in here and ask me for advice about marrying your teenage cousin?"

"Well when you say it that way it sounds rather bad."

Mary flipped her hair over her shoulder and laughed.

Edgar had missed that sound.

"It sounds bad because it is," she said as she poured them each a glass of wine.

It was quiet in the tavern, almost everyone else had left as the moon hung high in the sky above the shabby building.

"I know it is," Edgar says, frustrated. "Don't you think I know that? That's why I came to ask you for advice."

"Well," Mary said, raising her wineglass to her lips, "do you want to marry her?"

"No."

"Then there you go."

"Mary!"

Mary sighed then took a gulp of wine. Edgar joined her.

"If you don't marry her then that rich guy will, right?"

He nodded and drank more wine.

"Does she want to marry him?"

"No."

"And she does want to marry you?"

Beg for me.

Edgar saw Virginia for what she was, his cousin, his friend, something like a sister. The sister he never got to have. Whenever he and Virginia spent time together, reading stories, singing songs at the piano, even just staying up late and talking, he swore he could feel the spirit of his sister Rosalie. A girl who he never got to know. Rosalie could be dead now for all he knew. And Virginia was here, and she needed his help.

"Yes," he said. "Yes, she wants to marry me."

"Well, if it's her choice then that's all that matters isn't it?"

"If it were really about her choice we wouldn't even be having this conversation."

Mary paused, her rare, green eyes gazing into Edgar's. They were both hazy with drink. They were both getting lost in the late hours of the night.

"I can't marry her," Edgar whispered. "I love her, but not like that."

"You're a good man, Eddie."

"Please don't call me that."

"You have a big heart," Mary said, placing her hand on top of his. "You're addicted to caring about people. About the emotions of the whole world. You let yourself be haunted not just by your own sadness but by the sadness of everyone you care about. You're allowed to think of what would make you happy."

Edgar turned his hand over so Mary could slide her fingers between his.

"Come here," he said.

Mary smiled then pushed the wine glasses aside and crawled over the bar and into Edgar's lap.

"I've waited ten years to be kissed by you," she whispered.

"I'm sorry I'm so late."

"You're forgiven."

Edgar leaned forward and captured her mouth in a kiss.

The night melted around them and for the first time since his brother's death, he felt just the tiniest bit at ease.

* * *

Dearest cousin,

I have written to Maria and expressed my love for you and how I do not think it is wise to send you away to live with Nielson. I however cannot ask for your hand. You know we are not in love with each other and have lived as brother and sister these past few years. You are my closest friend, and my favorite person in this world, but if you marry me you will still be trapped, just in a different kind of cage. There is a whole world out there, cousin, I beg of you to go see it if you can.

I know Maria and Neilson want to convince you that you are uneducated because you haven't had proper schooling, but as you said yourself, they have no plans to provide you with an actual education. And as someone who has received one myself I must say that I find them rather overrated.

I have included a few hundred dollars in this letter, as much as I can spare. Come see me, Sissy. Or go somewhere else. Anywhere. Go on an adventure, and when you're done I will still be here, ready to hear all about it.

I wish you the best of luck in the world.
If anyone can survive its torments and toils,
I know it's you.

With all my love,
your friend, Edgar

* * *

Virginia never wrote back.

* * *

Edgar began visiting Mary regularly and soon he invited her to come home with him. The two shared a glass of brandy and crawled into bed together.

When they were finished with their bodies they dove into each other's minds. Mary asked him about his childhood, she asked about Boston and Baltimore. She asked about the inspiration behind all of his stories and poems.

"You've been reading my work?"

"What I can get my hands on, yes. Of course. Did you really think I wouldn't?"

Edgar answered her by crawling down between her legs.

He liked the sound of her moans almost as much as he loved the sound of her laugh.

Edgar wanted to ask Mary to marry him, but he knew she went home with other lovers and more importantly, he knew he wasn't in love with her.

He had only ever truly been in love once.

He was in love with Annabel, but he could never seem

to stay with her, this abominable reality always sucked him back in. If he could stay on that beach with her forever he would. But he was sentenced to the cold and lonely world of the living.

On Mary's birthday he gifted her a bundle of poems wrapped in ribbon the same shade as her eyes and held the words 'I love you.' On his tongue. He wondered if she wanted him to say them. He suspected she didn't. Their relationship to one another was safer this way.

In the middle of the dreary winter, Edgar was getting ready for bed when he heard a clattering sound in the front hall. He quickly surveyed all the corners of his room, they were barren of any shadows, and he wasn't even drunk. He sighed in relief, it was probably just the wind rattling the windows.

He pulled back the covers of his bed.

The clattering sound happened again. Closer to his room this time.

He gasped loudly as he looked at the door. A young woman, dressed all in black with hair the color of night and a mouth red as blood stood, in his doorway.

Edgar clutched a hand to his heart, wondering if he was finally dying. If the shadows of his mind had finally taken human shape and were coming to carry him away to hell.

"Who are you?" Edgar whispered. "What do you want with me?"

The woman opened her mouth and bloody teeth fell like candies, clattering onto the floor.

Edgar finally gave into his most base emotions.

He screamed.

He stumbled back, slamming himself against the wall as the bloodied woman continued to walk towards him. Her bloody mouth agape as teeth kept falling to the floor.

"Berenice?" He whispered.

The woman nodded, her mouth now devoid of any teeth.

Edgar wanted to cry.

He wanted to bash his head into the wall.

Anything to make this god-forsaken madness end.

A hand fell on his shoulder.

He looked to his side.

"Roderick?"

"Get a hold of yourself, man. Follow me."

Roderick grabbed Edgar's wrist and dragged him out the window. Edgar screamed again but instead of plummeting to their deaths they landed on the soft carpet of Roderick's library.

By the time Edgar had gotten to his feet Roderick was already at the door, holding two shovels.

"Come on," he said, "there's no time to waste."

Edgar didn't argue.

He took a shovel and the two men began their descent into the Usher Family Cemetery

The air was thick with despair and the stars were all blown out. Edgar followed Roderick deeper and deeper through the winding path of graves until they reached a large, ornate headstone.

"We dig?" Edgar asked.

Roderick nodded.

"We dig."

The two men said nothing as they dug and dug. Their brows became stained with dirt and the underside of their fingernails darkened so much that Edgar wondered if they would ever be clean again.

After half an hour—or a small eternity, Edgar wasn't quite sure—they reached the dreaded coffin. Edgar looked at Roderick who was staring at the coffin with eyes full of fear.

"Roderick, we can—"

Roderick lunged forward and opened the coffin.

It was empty.

He looked at Edgar, forlorn.

"If she's still alive, then who put this here? Who buried this beneath the earth?"

"I don't know," Edgar said.

Edgar looked up at the starless sky for a moment, searching for something; what, he wasn't sure. Inspiration, divine guidance, *something*.

He looked back down at the grave but found he was just staring at his bedroom floor.

He wiped his forehead, there was no dirt.

He looked at his nails, they were clean.

He searched the floor for Berenice's bloody teeth or Roderick's muddy footprints. There was nothing. He was completely, and utterly alone.

Chapter 6

Yet we met; and fate bound us together

New York City, 1839

Edgar checked with the Innkeeper to see if any post had arrived for him and felt his spirits sink yet again when he was told no.

His first collection of stories, *Tales of the Grotesque and Arabesque,* had been published over a month ago and he was yet to see a single dime of compensation for his work.

"Ulalume, will you tell me if anything comes later tonight?"

Ulalume, the Innkeeper's daughter, smiled and nodded.

"Of course, Edgar."

Edgar wrapped his coat around him and headed out into the bitter, January night.

He wandered aimlessly, too restless to sit in his room, but not quite weary enough to frequent a pub. The past few months the shadows had calmed down and he hadn't been visited again by Roderick or Berenice, so he'd lightened up on the drinking. He could never forget the hollowness of Henry's eyes when he came upon his dead body years ago; he didn't want someone to have to find him the same way.

So he wandered. Wandering helped him come up with new ideas for stories and poems. He was able to take the shadows and the sadness and craft them into something he could sell. Something he could make others feel.

His walks also helped him keep his thoughts off of who he was missing. Mary, Petronella, Henry, and Virginia. Sometimes he forgot that Petronella and Henry were gone. He would hear their voices in his dreams and wake thinking they would be waiting for him downstairs, or just around the corner. But they were never there. Everyday he woke up alone. And now every night he walked alone.

He found his way down streets he hadn't traveled before until he wandered up to a small alcove of a building with a small sign that read *Books*. He peered in the glass, it seemed to be open even though it was nearly midnight.

Inside was a small tavern full of laughing, chatting, loving poets and readers. Folks had wine and spirits in hand and someone was on a small stage in the corner playing a lively tune on the fiddle. Edgar took it all in, let the warmth of hearth fire, and the joy of the patrons wash away the cold from outside. He made his way to the bar where a hand-some, young, black man came over to take his order.

"Hi there," he said, "welcome to the Storytellers' Corner, what can I—"

The man's eyes grew wide and his words ceased. Edgar looked behind him, worried that the shadows had finally become visible to the outside world. But there was nothing there other than the same lively people as before.

"You're Edgar Allan Poe."

Edgar turned back around to look at the man who was now grinning.

"Pardon?"

"You are! You're him. I've seen your picture in the papers."

"Oh," Edgar said. He felt a nervous fluttering in his stomach. He had never been recognized before. "Yes, I am."

"Incredible," the man said. "I'm sorry if I'm overwhelming you, I just adore your work."

Edgar was dumbstruck.

"Thank you," he said, softly, somewhat in awe. "What's..." he coughed from the cold and the shock. "I mean...that is...do you have a favorite piece?"

"*Berenice* is my favorite story."

Edgar thought back to when Berenice came to his room, spitting her bloody teeth across his floor. He did his best to hide the horror the memory brought forth from being displayed on his face.

"Thank you," he said again; having no idea what else to say.

"But your poem *Alone* is the finest piece of writing I've ever read."

Edgar felt an arrow that had been lodged in his heart since the day Elmira disappeared from his life, finally beginning to dislodge.

"I..." Edgar felt tears begin to drampen his lashes. He reached in his pocket for a handkerchief and realized he hadn't brought one with him. So instead he rested his hand on the countertop and began to drum his fingers anxiously. "I've never..."

The man boldly reached out and placed his hand on top of Edgar's.

"From the same source I have not taken, my sorrows I could not awaken. My heart to joy—at the same tone. And all I loved, I loved alone."

Edgar felt tears begin to streak his face.

"You are truly a great poet, Mr. Poe. Has no one told you this before?"

Mary. Petronella. Henry. Virginia.

Elmira.

Why did he always doubt them? Because they were his family and friends. Because he felt they were obligated to say so. He worried they had just been lying the whole time.

But here was a stranger quoting his words back to him.

Words he wrote during some of his darkest hours.

A poem he had written in the wake of Petronella's death with thoughts of Elmira forever clouding his mind.

Literary critics at the time had said it was too bleak.

Confusing.

Meaningless.

Pretentious.

But it had meant more to him than all the rest.

"Thank you," Edgar said again, with more fervor this time. "No one has said that to me in quite some time."

The man squeezed his hand and smiled.

"What can I get you, Mr. Poe?"

"Whisky. On the rocks."

The man nodded.

"Coming right up."

He walked away to make his drink and Edgar was suddenly overcome with an all new fear.

He felt in his chest the way he had when he first met Elmira.

* * *

The Witching Hour had come again and Edgar was the last one in the tavern. He and the barkeep had talked and laughed the whole night through. Edgar had forgotten about his lost paycheck and his gray loneliness. He was warm and he felt happy for the first time in years.

"Wow," the man said, glancing at the window. "It's really coming down out there."

Edgar looked to see that the flurries from earlier had turned into an all out snowstorm, with wind roaring and rattling the windows.

"I'm sorry to have kept you," Edgar said, jumping to his feet and reaching into his coat for money.

The man stood still behind the counter and smiled at Edgar.

"Would you like to know my name?" He asked as Edgar fumbled in his pocket.

He froze and looked back at the man.

"Yes," Edgar said. "I would."

The man kept his eyes on Edgar's as he came out from behind the bar to stand in front of Edgar. He was much taller than Edgar—he towered above him with an impressive and intimidating stature. His relaxed smile remained as he looked down at the poet. It made Edgar feel at ease—a rarity.

"I'm Oscar."

He held out his hand.

Edgar took it in his.

Oscar pulled Edgar closer and leaned down to meet Edgar's lips in a kiss.

Edgar stiffened at first in fear and internal horror at what he was doing. But then Oscar wove his fingers with Edgar's and used his other hand to gently tangle his fingers in Edgar's hair and all sense of dread Edgar had felt just a moment before suddenly vanished. He leaned into Oscar's kiss, feeling a reckless passion coursing through his body.

He knew this was a crime.

They were different races.

They were the same sex.

In some states men hanged for this.

But Petronella had been the same. She had been so beautifully and boldly herself. And she had still shown such fear when she confided her truth in Edgar. But he hadn't loved her any less for it. She had been his best friend and he missed her with every waking breath.

If she were here with him she would tell him to give in to his heart.

Love isn't a sin.

Oscar and Edgar pulled apart and rested their foreheads together.

"Maybe," Edgar said softly, "we should go somewhere else."

He glanced at the window where a dark and dreary night soaked in snow lay beyond. It was unlikely anyone would walk by and discover them, but still fear of being caught clung to him.

Oscar went and locked the door then returned to Edgar and took his hand once more.

"Follow me."

Oscar led Edgar behind the bar to a small staircase in the back.

Upstairs was a small loft room with a bed, a desk, a chaise lounge, and a wood stove. There was also a small window at the far end where the snow could still be seen coming down.

"It's not much," Edgar said. "But it's mine."

Edgar turned to face Oscar.

"I've never..."

Oscar laughed and squeezed Edgar's hand.

"Yes, darling, that's a bit obvious."

"I knew a woman once who was…like you."

"How?" Oscar asked with another gentle laugh. "Was she black or a queer?"

"Both."

Oscar laughed again.

"I didn't realize the great poet was so worldly."

Edgar smiled, unsure of what to say.

"You don't have to do anything you don't want to," Oscar said.

Edgar looked at the bed in the corner of the room then back at Oscar. He looked into Oscar's warm eyes and bright smile.

Love isn't a sin.

"I want to," he said. "If you'll have me. Inexperienced lover as I am."

Oscar twirled a lock of Edgar's hair around his finger.

"*Have* you ever made love, Mr. Poe?"

Edgar felt the flap of butterfly wings beat against his ribcage.

"Edgar," he breathed. "Call me Edgar."

Oscar stepped closer and wrapped his arm around Edgar's hips, pulling Edgar against him.

"Have you ever made love, Edgar?"

"Only to women."

Oscar smiled again.

"It's not so different."

Edgar tilted his head back so he could keep gazing into Oscar's eyes.

"Will you show me?"

Oscar leaned forward and kissed him again.

"Gladly," he murmured against his mouth.

What are you so afraid of?

Edgar sat up in bed.

He didn't know where he was.

He began to panic.

But then he heard the sigh of exhaling breath. He turned and saw Oscar sound asleep beside him and the memories of the past few hours came rushing back. He looked to the window, the snow was still falling so hard that you could barely see the sun trying to rise against it.

Afraid of your neck snapping for being a filthy sodomite.

Edgar practically fell out of bed at the sound of the voice.

"Who's there?" He whispered.

John Allan was right to be disgusted by you.

"My father enslaved people," Edgar hissed defiantly at the voice. "His opinion doesn't matter."

You wished to marry a child.

Images of Virginia flashed in his mind. He grabbed his head and willed the voice to stop.

"We were just friends," he whispered helplessly. "I know she was a child."

You and Elmira were both children and even she didn't love you.

"Stop. Please stop," Edgar begged.

You are a pitiful, unloveable thing.

Edgar fell over on his side and sobbed as the voice kept attacking him.

The man in bed lied to you. You are a terrible writer. Other writers make a fortune off their work. Yet you still live in poverty.

Edgar lifted his head slightly. He realized the voice was coming from beneath the floorboards.

Virginia loathes you. That's why she never writes to you. Petronella didn't even want you by her side when she died.

Your birth parents didn't even want you. Your brother doesn't even miss you.

Edgar laid flat on his back, closed his eyes, and screamed. He didn't care who he woke. He didn't care how mad he seemed, he couldn't stand another moment of this torment.

"Edgar. Come on, man, pull yourself together."

Edgar kept screaming.

Why hadn't Oscar awoken yet?

"Edgar, come. Let me help you, friend."

Edgar opened his eyes.

There was someone standing over him, holding out their hand.

"Roderick?"

"Come on," Roderick Usher said again. "You can't stay here."

Edgar took Roderick's hand.

When he was standing again they were no longer in Oscar's loft.

They were on Anabel's beach.

Roderick was gone.

"Annabel?" Edgar called out. "Annabel!"

"Up here!"

Edgar looked up to see Annabeth standing on top of one of the rocky cliffs that looked out over the ocean.

"Come watch the sunrise with me, Edgar."

Edgar made his way up the cliffside until he reached Annabel.

"Hello, my love," she said with a sweet smile.

She came over to him and stood on tiptoe to kiss him. He wrapped his arms around her waist and pulled her in close. The kiss consumed them. It was ravenous and wild. By the time they broke apart Edgar was breathing heavily.

Annabel put her hand over his heart.

It was racing.

"What's wrong?" She asked.

"I truly have gone mad," he said. "I've made this all up in my mind. It's as if I cannot cope with the real world so I created a different one inside my head."

He went and stood at the edge of the cliff.

He looked at the sun cresting the ocean.

It all looked so real.

He could feel the wind and taste the salty air.

So how could it not be real?

"You didn't make me up, Edgar," Annabel said. "I was here before you. And I shall be here when you're gone."

Edgar looked back at her.

"Where? Where do you go when I'm gone?"

"The beach isn't the only thing there is beyond your world. It is just where yours meets mine. It is as far as I can go right now, and it is as far as you can come."

"Where?" He stepped back towards her. "Where do you come from, Annabel?"

She shook her head.

"I can't explain that right now. You're not ready."

"But what about the others? The characters from my stories?"

"What about them?"

"Surely you don't mean to tell me that Berenice, and Nesace, and Roderick Usher are all real."

"You've seen them and spoken to them. What else do they need to be real?"

"Substance!"

"Athena was birthed from the mind of Zeus."

"What?" Edgar said, flustered and overburdened. "I am not a god, Annabel. Stop talking nonsense!"

"I'm not," Annabel insisted. She reached out and took his hand in hers. It was shaking. "It makes sense you've created a world inside your mind. That's what storytellers do. You're a storyteller, Edgar."

"I'm a madman!"

"You fancy yourself mad?"

Edgar nodded.

Annabel scoffed. "Impossible."

"How?" Edgar begged. "How is it impossible that I am mad?

"Because madmen know nothing. And you, Edgar Allan Poe, know everything."

Edgar looked into Annabel's ocean eyes, searching for proof that she was real. That she wasn't a figment of his insanity, or a specter from another life.

He began to shake harder as the tears started to fall. He reached up and took her face in his hands.

"I love you," he whispered.

Annabel gripped his wrists, holding on to him as firmly as he did her.

"I live with no other thought than to love and be loved by you."

* * *

Edgar woke up with Oscar's arm around his waist and the soft sound of snow falling outside.

But he could still taste the salt of the sea on his tongue.

* * *

"Well?" Edgar asked when Oscar placed the paper down between them on the chaise.

Oscar smirked like a sly alleycat before leaning forward and kissing his lover.

"I think it's the most brilliant story you've written yet."

"Truly?" Edgar asked between kisses.

"Yes. Truly. Mark my words, Mr. Poe, readers will be talking about *The Fall of the House of Usher* for hundreds of years.

Chapter 7

They who dream by day are cognizant of many things which escape those who dream only by night

New York City, 1841

"Edgar, someone's at the door!" Oscar called from where he was soaking in the tub.

Edgar looked up from his desk and sighed. "I'm busy!"

But Oscar ignored him. Edgar sighed more dramatically so that Oscar could hear. He heard the soft, sweet sound of Oscar's laugh and shook his head, laughing to himself.

He opened the door.

Virginia was standing outside, freshly fallen snowflakes sticking to her dark lashes.

"Hello, Eddie."

He felt his heart drop down the rafters of his ribcage and clatter at the bottom of his stomach.

"Sissy?"

She gave a weak smile and nodded.

"Can I come in?"

Edgar nodded, dumbfounded, and stepped back to let her in.

"Can I get you something?" He asked, as she made her way into the small sitting room. "Tea? Coffee? Whisky?"

She chuckled softly. "It's a bit early for that. Some tea would be fine."

He rushed to get her some, his hands shaking the whole time. As he brought it over to her, the cup rattling against the saucer in his unsteady hands, he noticed Virginia looking up at the ceiling.

He looked up.

And realized.

Oscar liked to sing when he took a bath, and the sound of his melodic voice was carrying through the floorboards.

"Do you live with someone else?"

Edgar panicked.

Virginia had been gone from his life for so long, what would she think of him? She was no longer a little girl who idolized him as some great writer who could do no real wrong. She was a young woman with her own opinions and ideals about life. He hadn't the slightest inkling of how she would feel about him living in such a way.

"Yes," he said, his throat scratchy with nerves. "My friend Oscar lives with me."

"I see." Virginia sipped her tea as Edgar sat down across from her.

The two sat in silence for several moments, the only sound in the house was that of Oscar singing an old lullaby.

"I have something of yours," Virginia said, finally. She reached into the small bag she'd brought with her and pulled out a copy of a recent journal Edgar had been published in. She unfolded it and placed it on the table between them. She pointed to his story, *Eleanora.* "This isn't about me."

Edgar looked down at the story.

A short, little tale of love. So unlike the horror's he had been writing about for so long.

"Yes, it is," he insisted. "You told me to write about you one day."

She sighed.

"You can pretend the character in the story is your cousin but we both know better. You talk of this Eleanora as someone you met during the third lustrum of her life. I was still a small child when you came to live with Mother and me."

"I changed a few details."

"Eddie, we are not in love. We never have been. Who is the story about?"

"It's about Elmira."

Edgar and Virginia turned to see Oscar standing at the foot of the stairs, his dark skin glistening with water droplets.

He looked like a God.

Edgar felt wonderfully on fire looking at him.

"Hello," Oscar said. "You must be Edgar's cousin, Virginia. I've heard a great deal about you." Oscar walked over and held his hand out to Virginia. "I'm Oscar."

Virginia shook Oscar's hand then glanced back at Edgar.

Edgar felt sick.

Maria Clemm had been as racist as John Allan. He had no idea if Virginia had inherited her mother's hateful ideals when it came to human rights. He, himself, had to unlearn a childhood raised in the shadow of John Allan's vile ways.

Edgar loved his cousin like a sister.

But if she would not accept Oscar then he would say goodbye to her forever.

"Won't you join us?" Virginia said to Oscar.

Oscar smiled.

"I would be delighted. Let me go get a cup of tea."

Oscar left for the kitchen. Edgar looked at Virginia in true shock.

"I am not my mother," Virginia said—answering his unspoken question. "Just as you are not your father. I am also not a fool."

"I don't know what you mean, Virginia."

"He's your lover."

Edgar felt her words stab him in the chest, his blood pooling in his lap, dripping down his chest, drops falling into his tea.

"Don't be ridiculous," he scoffed, but he knew how unconvincing his voice sounded.

"Edgar, there was a time when I knew you better than anyone. You were my best friend, and my hero. I can see in your eyes when your heart is so full of love."

"I..." Edgar searched for the right words, but could not find a single one.

He turned to look back for Oscar, but he was still gone in the kitchen.

Edgar looked back to where Virginia sat across from him and he nearly screamed in horror.

Roderick Usher was sitting next to her on the couch.

"You should trust her, my man," Roderick said in words only Edgar could hear. "She is your family. Hold onto that. Hold on to her."

"Virginia," Edgar said, "tell me why you came here. Surely it wasn't to badger me about the details of a story I wrote."

Virginia finished her tea.

"You're right. I came to take you up on the offer you made me years ago."

"You want to stay with me?"

She nodded. "Mother would see me wed, as would polite society. I have no desire for such a thing."

"Why not?"

"Because I am like you, Edgar."

"Virginia..."

"Her name is Frances."

"It's a good thing you came here then," Oscar said as he sauntered back into the room and sat down next to Virginia. "Welcome to our house of sin, Miss Virginia Clemm."

Virginia smiled and Edgar realized he had nearly forgotten how beautiful a sight it was.

Virginia's smile was the sun itself.

Winter melted away with the spread of her lips.

Roderick raised an eyebrow at Edgar, smiled, and vanished.

Edgar looked at Oscar, who was smiling as well.

Edgar thought of Elmira for a moment.

Then of Annabel.

The ocean.

The past.

"You can stay with us, Sissy."

Her smile became a grin.

* * *

A sound almost like the ticking of a clock woke Edgar from his sleep that night.

He sat up in bed, looking all around the small bedroom he shared with Oscar.

He glanced at Oscar, fast asleep; undisturbed by the sound.

Edgar got up, put on his slippers and dressing gown, and descended the stairs. Virginia was asleep, curled up on the couch, buried beneath every blanket they could spare, but she still shivered against the bitter winter winds shaking the small house.

Edgar tended to the fire and added his and Oscar's coats to the blanket pile on top of Virginia and then headed to the kitchen, searching for the source of the ticking-like sound.

When he pushed open the kitchen door he had to swallow a scream.

A giant ax was swinging back and forth from the ceiling, like a pendulum.

Edgar felt his heart begin to race.

"Roderick?" he called out in a whisper. "Roderick, are you here?"

The back door swung open and Roderick barged into the house in a flurry of snow and wind. He looked at the swinging ax and then to Edgar.

"Come, my friend, this is no place for you."

Edgar took Roderick's hand and followed him out the door.

When they walked through they were no longer in the midst of a snowy New York City night, but in the confines of Roderick's study. The fire was high in the hearth, and Roderick had already set out two glasses of wine on the table between the armchairs.

But there was someone sitting in one of them.

Madeline.

Roderick's sister stood, smiled, and walked over to Edgar.

She kissed his cheek and wrapped him in a warm embrace; her thin frame melding perfectly to his.

"Thank you for keeping Roderick company," she said. "You are a good friend."

With that she walked past him and Roderick, out into

the hall, the giant oak doors swinging shut behind her. Edgar looked to Roderick.

"Is she well?"

"Who?"

"Madeline, your sister."

Roderick's eyes grew wide.

"She was here?"

"Yes, didn't you see her?"

The light in Roderick's eyes dimmed.

"I never see her anymore, Poe."

Roderick stalked over to the armchairs, collapsed in one, and reached for the glass of wine.

"Roderick," Edgar said, his voice soft against the crackling sound of the fire, "is Madeline real?"

"What a ridiculous question. Of course she's real."

"And what about you? Are you real? Or are you just all in my head?"

Roderick took a gulp of wine.

"I'm as real as the wind, Poe."

Edgar felt tears brush his cheeks. He shook his head.

"But you're not. You're a character from a story I wrote. Just like Berenice. Just like all the gods for Al Aaraff. You're all just characters I dreamed up. I imagined you. I imagined this room. I created it all in my mind. I understand that. What I don't understand is why you all haunt me after the stories have been written. Why do you all haunt me so?"

"Because," Roderick said, "you let us."

* * *

"Edgar! Edgar, wake up!"

Edgar opened his eyes.

He was curled in a ball on the kitchen floor, Virginia was kneeling beside him.

"Virginia?"

"Yes, Eddie, I'm here."

He sat up and fell into her arms. She held him tight, holding him close, his head resting against her heart. He had forgotten how good it felt to have Virginia close.

"I fear I've gone mad, Sissy."

Virginia smoothed down his wild hair.

"You haven't gone mad."

He leaned back, his eyes met hers.

"I see things, Virginia. I have for years. Since I was an adolescent. Characters and creatures. They don't just haunt my dreams, but my waking hours as well. Just now there was a giant, deadly ax swinging across the kitchen. And then I was in the house of Roderick Usher. I see them, Virginia. The monsters I make come to me and I cannot seem to banish them."

Virginia sat silently for several moments, just staring at her cousin.

"Is that all?"

Edgar balked at her.

"Because I knew all that already," she said. "So did Henry."

"You did? But I—I just—"

"Did you really think your family loved and cared for you so little that we didn't take stock of who you really were? You are not some great secret, Edgar Allan Poe. We knew you as well as you knew us."

"So you knew? You knew all this time that I'm a madman?"

Virginia sighed. "If that is how you wish to refer to yourself, then yes. But that's certainly not the word I would use."

"What word would you use?"

"Brilliant."

Edgar glared at her.

"I mean it. So what if you can see things the rest of us cannot? Why should that make it any less real?"

"Because it isn't!"

"It's real to you."

"Because I'm insane, Virginia! What about that don't you understand!"

"The part where you loathe yourself."

Silence fell over them like snow.

"You've suffered so much tragedy in your life that you've come to think you deserve it. Your mind has played some nasty tricks on you—it has convinced you into thinking that how you think and feel is a defect; a failure. But you are the farthest thing from a failure that there is. You want to fancy yourself mad? Well I fancy that is absurd. Madmen know nothing."

"That's what Annabel said," he whispered.

"So write about it."

"You don't want to know who Annabel is?" He asked in genuine confusion.

Virginia smiled and shrugged.

"I'm sure I'll read about her one day."

"You really don't believe me to be mad?" He asked.

Virginia shook her head.

"You see the world differently than most. You have the power to bring stories to life. To make worlds out of words on a page. That is not madness. It's magic."

Chapter 8

You fancy me mad? Madmen know nothing.

Baltimore Maryland, 1842

"I think we should get married."

Edgar and Oscar looked up from where they were sharing a copy of *The Tempest*. They had just reached the part where Ariel asks Prospero if he loves them.

"Virginia, no."

"People are starting to talk."

"No, they're not," Edgar said, defensively.

But he knew she was right. Ever since the trio had moved back to Baltimore, into the house Maria Clemm had left them, the people in the neighborhood had begun to whisper about them. Even though it was the North, people still clutched their pearls at the idea of an unwed woman living with two men, even if one of them was her cousin.

And Edgar knew they whispered about him and Oscar.

What they were to each other.

The way that society saw them as too similar, and the way they saw them as too different. There was no winning in this world, Edgar feared, when it came to a love like theirs.

"If we wed then no one will ask questions anymore.

They will be forced to accept the story we choose to tell them."

"And what story is that, Miss Virginia?" Oscar asked.

"Edgar will be my husband and you our friend."

"You mean your servant?"

"No. If we are married then no one need concern themselves with what we do beneath

our own roof as husband and wife."

"Virginia, you're a..." Edgar started, catching himself.

"A sapphic? Yes, Edgar, I know. This marriage will conceal mine and Frances' relationship as well. This union will protect us all."

Edgar looked at Oscar.

"I fear she might be right," Oscar said.

Virginia smirked.

"I usually am."

* * *

On his wedding night, Edgar went to bed with Oscar as Virginia snuck off to Frances' house.

"Come, my love," Oscar said from where he lay sprawled across the sheets in nothing but a nightshirt.

Edgar removed his dressing robe and made his way to his lover. He stopped at the end of the bed and then got down on his knees.

Oscar laughed. "What are you doing?"

Edgar held his hands out and Oscar dutifully slipped his into place against Edgar's; weaving their fingers up like a perfect pair of bows.

"I love you, Oscar," Edgar whispered.

Oscar smiled.

"I love you too."

Edgar relinquished one hand to reach under the bed; he pulled out a small, black box.

Inside was a ring.

A simple, silver band.

He could not afford anything more.

Oscar inhaled soft, and sharp.

"Oscar, to put it quite plainly—I adore you. Before I met you I had only known heartbreak. I thought I understood what it felt like to fall in love; but one kiss from you proved me wrong. Every other flight of fancy in love I'd felt until that moment paled in comparison. There is nothing like being loved by you. And there is no greater joy than loving you."

"I know no church would ever recognize our union. I know that if there is a god above, that he himself might deem this kind of love a sin. But I have never cared much for god. So let the stars and moon above tonight bear witness; Oscar, will you marry me?"

Oscar had tears in his eyes.

His smile beamed brighter than the sun.

"Of course I will, you fool."

* * *

Edgar awoke later that night, the winds outside blowing so loudly it shook the whole house. He wrapped himself in his dressing robe once more and descended the stairs to his study. He lit a candle stub, dipped his quill in the well, and began to write.

Then he heard the ticking sound.

More like a beating.

It was coming from the floor.

He got down on hands and knees and pressed his cheek

to the cool floorboard.

Sinner.

A demonic voice hissed from the floor.

Edgar jumped back.

No, he thought, *not again.*

He got up and ran out of the house to see Virginia coming up the front path.

"Edgar? What is it? What's wrong?"

He couldn't find the words. No matter how many times someone he loved told him it was okay to suffer the mental maladies he did, he always felt such shame in the moment.

One look at her husband, and Virginia knew what was wrong.

She raced over to him and began to guide him back into the house.

He cried out. Begged her not to make him go back.

"Edgar, please, you'll wake the neighbors."

"What's wrong?" Oscar asked, coming down the stairs.

"The visions," Virginia said.

Oscar rushed over to the man that was also his husband in the eyes of the stars, and tried to soothe him. But Edgar was slipping away.

Edgar!

"Annabel?"

"Who's Annabel?" Oscar asked.

Virginia shook her head hopelessly.

Edgar, this way!

Virginia and Oscar tried again to guide him into the house, and this time he let them, because beyond the door was no longer the shabby home with tormenting voices in the floorboards, but the beautiful beach where his Annabel Lee waited for him.

The one he loved with a love that was more than a love.

His Annabel Lee.

"Annabel!" He cried out in relief as he crashed into her arms with the waves.

The water tugged at them, the salt staining their skin.

He kissed her and for a wonderful, fleeting moment, his troubles washed away.

"Are you alright?" She asked, taking his face in her hands.

He studied her.

Her pale, moon skin. Her rich brown eyes. Her button nose. Her flowing hair that was such a dark brown it was nearly black as the night sky where the stars always shone on this beach.

This sanctuary.

No voices that taunted him.

No monsters of his mind to torment him.

There was simply Annabel, and the ocean, and peace.

And yet—

"Annabel, what are you?"

Annabel sighed.

"You ask that so often."

"I need to know. Did I make you up? Are you all inside my mind?"

"Edgar, I'm not inside your mind."

"Then where am I! Where is *here*? How are you able to come to me when I'm trapped with Roderick, or lost in reality? What is this beach? Why are we the only two people on it? What's beyond the cliffs? Where are you when I'm gone?"

He was hysterical.

Annabel smiled and the heavens sang.

"Edgar," she said softly; lovingly. "You already know all of that."

He breathed deeply. The salty air invading his lungs.

"Are you a ghost?" He whispered.

"Oh, Edgar, of course I am."

"How...how did I find you?"

"You will remember when the time is right."

"But," he pleaded, "why can't I be with you always? Why won't you come with me? Haunt me! Please! I just cannot bear the world without you."

"You're married, my darling," she said, stroking her thumb down the curve of his jaw. "There are people who love you back in the world of the living."

"So are we in the afterlife? Is that what this place is?"

"This is a place in between."

"Annabel, please, take me with you. Take me away from the shadows."

She took his hands in hers, brought them to her lips, and placed a gentle kiss to his knuckles.

"My darling, Edgar, the day will come when we will stay together. But I hope it won't be for a long time."

Then a wave crashed over them both and when Edgar reached the surface he was back in his bed, Oscar and Virginia by his side.

* * *

Virginia set down the copy of *The Tell Tale Heart* Edgar had given her when he'd gotten home from the magazine that evening. She grinned.

"It's brilliant," she said, her eyes all aglow.

"Truly? It's not too gruesome?"

"Oh, it's far too gruesome, and that's why I adore it. And I'm glad you finally wrote about me."

Edgar chuckled. "What do you mean?"

"Madmen know nothing, Mr. Poe," his wife said with a mischievous smirk.

"Alright, maybe I took a little inspiration from my Sissy, but believe it or not you were not the first person to question my sanity."

"I never questioned it, dear cousin, I always knew you were wonderfully insane."

The two laughed and drank tea and for a lovely little while, there wasn't a shadow in sight

Chapter 9

*Deep into that darkness peering,
long I stood there, wondering,
fearing, dreaming dreams no
mortal ever dared to dream before.*

Newark Delaware, 1844

The trio entered the tavern, soaked from the rainstorm outside.

"I'll see about getting us a room," Edgar said.

"And Oscar and I will see about getting us some hot cider."

"Make it strong cider," Edgar said, rubbing his forehead where a splitting headache was taking over.

Virginia nodded, patted his shoulder, and led Oscar to the bar.

There were a few odd glances thrown the trio's way, but for the most part the Delawarians minded their own business; sipping ales and telling stories. Someone was in the corner of the room playing an organ and the rain was pattering against the windows in nearly perfect time to the music.

At the desk the clerk rented Edgar two rooms. One for him and his wife and one for their companion.

Edgar rejoined his friends and the three quickly drowned themselves in hot, hard cider.

"This trek to New York is proving to be quite arduous," Oscar said. "Remind me again why we're bothering?"

"Because," Virginia said, "Edgar had to go and get a job like a responsible adult."

"Edgar? Responsible? Surely you're mistaken."

The three continued to laugh through the night until the moon was high in the sky and they all slinked off to bed. Virginia followed Edgar into his room and the two remained together for about half an hour, sitting in a comfortable silence; the kind that can only be achieved between two people who are completely at home with each other.

After the half hour came and went, Virginia pretended to leave to use the bathroom, and Oscar came into the room in her stead, pressing the other room's key into her hand as they passed each other in the hall.

Oscar smiled a mischievous grin as he crawled into bed with Edgar. Edgar kissed him, wrapping his arms around his strong shoulders and holding him close.

"Do you ever dream of a world where we can fully be ourselves?" Oscar asked in the quiet, night air. "Because I do. More often than usual anymore. I dream of walking down the busy city streets of New York City with your hand in mine for all the world to see. I dream of a wedding where I can kiss you before the eyes of god and a room full of our friends and family applaud our happiness. I dream of growing old with you."

Edgar ran his hand down Oscar's cheek.

"We will grow old together."

Edgar reached under Oscar's shirt and took out the chain he always wore. Edgar wore a matching one, each holding their wedding bands.

"You're my husband," Edgar whispered. "Till death do us part and all that."

"Surely even death could not separate me from the Master of the Macabre."

Edgar laughed and the two lovers kissed.

As the night went on and the candles burned low, Edgar held his husband close and murmured against the soft hair on his head.

"You may forget, but let me tell you this, someone in some future time will think of us."

"Hmmm," Oscar sighed against Edgar's chest. "Sappho."

Edgar looked to the corners of the room, there were so many shadows, and the eye of the old man from his story stared back at him. The eye saw him for what he truly was in the eyes of the world.

Sinner.

Heathen.

Madman.

Edgar shook his head.

He thought of Petronella. How he missed her. He wished so terribly she was here for these times of immense self doubt to guide him through his grief and self-cruelty.

But Petronella was gone from this world.

Edgar hoped wherever death led, it led to somewhere kinder.

A place where everyone knows that love isn't a sin.

"I am not a sinner," Edgar whispered to the old man in the shadows. "Love is not a sin."

The old man laughed and stepped back into the shadows. Edgar sighed in relief and then gave in to the blissful release of sleep.

* * *

The next morning the rain was still too heavy to travel.

"We could walk to the train station," Virginia offered.

"I am not making you walk in this weather," Edgar said.

"You're not making me, I'm offering."

"No," he said. "We can wait one more day."

He didn't want to tell Virginia the real reason he didn't want to walk to the station. It had nothing to do with the weather, Virginia was a Marylander, he knew she could handle more than a little rain. But her eyes had become sunken these past few months, and her breathing had gotten short. He'd seen the same signs in Petronella in the months leading up to the end.

He would not exert his best friend for the sake of quick travel.

He would not risk her to get to New York on time.

No, their travel could wait.

They stayed in the tavern all day, reading, and occasionally Edgar scribbled into an old, pocket notebook some rogue phrases that flitted across his mind. The day turned into night and their mugs of tea turned into mugs of ale and the soft spoken tavern became rowdy again.

Too rowdy.

Some men who should've stayed in the South came in.

Men like John Allan.

The men took one look at the trio and the hatred Edgar had been constant witness to growing up burned in their eyes.

"Let's go," Edgar whispered.

Virginia and Oscar quickly got to their feet and followed after Edgar as he went to lead them to the stairs that led to their rooms.

But of course the men stopped them.

"Woah, hold on there," the biggest one of the men said,

putting a hand on Edgar's chest. "You're that crazy writer, ain't ya? It's him, ain't it fellas? Edgar Allan Poe. The madman himself."

"My husband isn't mad," Virginia said, grabbing onto Edgar's arm. "They're just stories. Now if you'll please excuse us, gentlemen, we must be getting to bed. We have an early train to catch tomorrow."

The men ignored her.

Their eyes landed on Oscar.

Edgar fought the burning desire to reach out for his husband.

"And what the hell do we have here?"

The man spit at Oscar.

He spoke an unforgivable word.

Edgar punched him.

Virginia cried out and Oscar reached for him, but one of the other men shoved Oscar back, sending him toppling over a table. The first man tried to hit Edgar back, but Edgar had spent his entire adolescence dodging John Allan's fists; a drunken racist was no match for him.

Edgar swerved from the man's fist, grabbed an empty bottle from a nearby table, smashed

it over the edge and held the shard out in front of him; positioning himself between Oscar and Virginia, and the vile men before him.

"Back up," Edgar said through his bared teeth.

The man looked at Edgar and then just laughed.

"You really are a crazy drunk. Guess all the stories are true."

Virginia grabbed Edgar's hand and took the shard of glass from it.

His palm was red as the mask of death.

"You're right," Edgar said to the man. "I am mad."

He held tight to Virginia's hand, looked at Oscar and nodded towards the stairs.

Again the three tried to pass.

And this time the man's fist did hit its mark when he swung.

Knocking Edgar to the floor with a sickening thud.

And Oscar didn't think.

He hit the man back.

The tavern went silent.

Edgar looked up through his bloody vision in horror.

Virginia inhaled sharply, trying not to cry.

Edgar scrambled to his feet, took Oscar's hand, and dragged him to the stairs with Virginia on their heels.

They all locked themselves in the same room.

Their panicked breaths were the only sound.

"I have to go," Oscar whispered.

"What?" Edgar and Virginia said.

"They'll call the police. I cannot be found."

"It was self defense," Virginia said, hopelessly.

"I hit a white man, Ginny."

Virginia began to cry.

"I hate this world," she whispered.

Oscar pulled Virginia into his arms and held her while she cried.

He kissed her forehead.

He packed his bag and headed for the window that led out to the low, slanted roof.

"No!" Edgar grabbed his hand, holding him in place on the windowsill. Oscar looked into his husband's eyes, and for once Edgar did not feel ashamed of his tears. "No," Edgar whispered. "We will go together."

"This is a small town," Oscar said. "It will be easy for the cops to spot the black man traveling with the Poes."

"Oscar, please" Edgar begged. "Please. Please don't go. I love you so much. Please stay. Please stay with me."

"I will meet you in New York City," Oscar whispered.

Edgar shook his head.

"I know you're lying."

Oscar smiled the smile of a soldier who knows he's lost the war.

They both knew it was too beautiful to last.

They were too ahead of their time.

"Someone in some future time," Edgar said.

"Will think of us," Oscar finished.

"Oscar," Edgar said, "you can't go. You're my home."

Oscar reached up and pressed his palm against Edgar's cheek.

"And you, my love," Oscar whispered, "are my heart."

Oscar leaned forward and kissed Edgar.

Edgar wept as he kissed him back.

And then he was gone.

Edgar crashed to the floor.

Virginia rushed to his side and took him in her arms.

When the cops came banging on their door an incredibly short while later all they found was the madman Poe in the arms of his young wife.

Another wild rumor for all the critics and gossip mongers.

Another stitch in the torn up tapestry of his heart.

"Never," Edgar whispered to Virginia late in the night as they laid side by side in bed, on top of the covers, both unable to sleep. "Never will I feel whole again."

"I loved him too," Virginia said. "But we still have each other, Edgar."

"And you have Frances," Edgar said, keeping his eyes on the ceiling.

"Edgar," Virginia said, wishing she had more powerful words to say.

"Never, never, nevermore will my heart heal."

And Virginia knew it was true.

She held her husband's hand.

And the shadows consumed him.

* * *

A rapping on the window woke Edgar from his sleep. He looked all around the room, there was only darkness and the soft sound of Virginia's breathing.

He lit a taper and began to inspect the corners.

Hunting through the darkness like a chasseur.

There was nothing.

It was but a rapping in his mind.

He moved back to the bed and the rapping sounded again.

He looked to the window.

A raven was perched outside.

Its beady, black, ominous eyes bore into Edgar's.

Edgar shook his head and the bird ruffled its feathers.

"No," Edgar whispered. "This is only a dream. Everything in this madness is a malady of my mind. You are not real."

Nevermore.

Edgar dropped the candle and the light went out.

In all his years living inside his ailing mind, never had anything spoken that shouldn't have.

Roderick was a man; men can speak.

Hearts can beat.

Ghosts can scream.

But birds cannot talk.

Nevermore.

Edgar rushed to the window and opened it. The bird flew in.

"What!" He yelled, not caring if he woke Virginia. Not caring if he woke the whole tavern. "I did not think you up! You are not a character from any of my writings. So what are you, devil? Who has sent you? Why have you come?"

Silly, foolish, Poe, the bird whispered through its beak. *I have always been with you.*

Edgar's knees practically gave out.

He gripped the bedpost to remain upright.

I am the darkness inside you. I am your still-beating heart. Your worries. Your fears. I am the ever-present knowledge that there is nothing for you here in this world. You were damned from birth ;every waking moment since you have simply been trying to fight the inevitable.

"Good God," Edgar whispered. "Deliver me from this evil."

There is no God. There is only darkness. Only truth. Only submission. Submit to your base urges, Poe. End your suffering.

Edgar gazed on at the winged beast in absolute holy horror.

Then a door appeared.

He recognized it.

* * *

"Hello, Poe," Roderick said as Edgar walked into his study.

"Hello, Usher," Edgar said.

Roderick handed Edgar a glass of wine. Edgar took it gladly.

The two men sat in front of the fire and listened to the wind blow furiously outside.

"What's wrong?" Roderick asked, finally.

"My husband has left."

"Your husband?"

Edgar nodded.

"I didn't realize you were a sodomite," Roderick said.

Edgar laughed coldly.

"I didn't either for a long time. But I love women too. Suppose I'm only half a sinner in that way." Edgar's drunk mind was beginning to take hold of his thoughts and his tongue. "I love women. But all the women I love die. My mother. My foster mother. My friends. And my wife, she is ill. I can see that she doesn't have long."

"I am sorry for that," Roderick said in earnest.

Edgar nodded solemnly, gazing into the flickering fire.

"I think the death of a beautiful woman is unquestioningly the most poetical topic in the world."

"That's tragic," Roderick said.

Edgar looked at his old friend.

"Is not the death of Madeline poetical to you?"

"I am not a poet."

"And Madeline is not dead."

"No," Roderick said. "Not really."

"She's just an idea, isn't she?" Edgar said. "There never really was a Madeline. You don't have a sister. You've been alone in this house all these years, you just made her up to ease your loneliness. You created her in your mind just as I created you in mine."

Roderick was silent.

"Admit it, Roderick. Admit to me that you're not real. That I truly am mad."

"Just because you made me up doesn't make me any less real."

"Of course it does!" Edgar shouted, jumping to his feet.

Roderick looked up at him, his face completely placid of any emotion.

It infuriated Edgar.

"I am real to you."

Edgar screamed. He threw his wineglass into the fire and knocked over the chair he was sitting in. He raged until he was short of breath and weak in the bones.

He fell to his knees before Roderick.

"You are real to me," Edgar whispered. "You're my best friend."

"I know, Poe," Roderick said. "And you are mine."

"I'm entirely mad."

"Perhaps," Roderick said. "But most brilliant people are."

* * *

Edgar spent the entire train ride to New York scribbling away in his notebook.

I am real to you.

"Edgar?" Virginia asked, nudging his shoulder.

Her voice sounded to him like it was coming from underwater as he kept writing:

Once upon a midnight dreary, while I pondered weak and weary...

"Edgar!"

Edgar pulled his mind from the reverie of writing to look at his wife.

"Where are you, Eddie?" She whispered.

"You're a million miles away."
I was never really here.

Chapter 10

Here I opened wide the door, darkness there and nothing more.

New York City, 1845

Oscar never returned. Virginia tried to soothe Edgar and comfort him, claiming that perhaps Oscar had gotten delayed, or lost, and would be there any day now.

Frances came to visit Virginia and all the papers and gossipers speculated that she was Edgar's mistress. He and Virginia didn't care. It only made them feel safer in their secrets.

Edgar continued to work on a long poem that had been haunting his mind since Newark.

Other writings of his reached publication but his hand always twitched and itched, wishing to return to the epic poem. He knew deep inside of him that this one was different than all the rest.

It was going to mean more.

Because it hurt the most.

Virginia's coughing worsened.

Frances would share knowing looks with Edgar when Virginia wasn't in the room.

Neither one of them wanted to accept that they must soon prepare for the worst.

* * *

Frances returned to Baltimore, and the rumors of her and Edgar went with her.

* * *

On a late night in January Edgar came home with a copy of *The Evening Mirror.*

He went to Virginia's room in their small apartment and placed it on her bedside. She was still fast asleep; she slept most hours of the night and day now, but Edgar didn't mind. If sleeping kept her alive then so be it.

He had circled his new poem in pencil and left it for her to find.

The Raven.

He went out to the kitchen and took a bottle of laudanum from a top cabinet.

He drank the whole thing.

His greatest poem; a suicide note.

* * *

"No," a voice boomed nearby. "Poe, my man, get up this instant."

And then there were fingers down his throat.

Edgar wretched and gagged as he vomited up all of the poison-like drink he'd downed not twenty minutes ago. He wiped at his tear-streaked face and looked to see Roderick kneeling beside him.

"Don't be a fool," Roderick said. "Don't let this world best you."

Edgar just stared at his fictitious friend.

"How?" He asked. "If you're not really real, how can you save me?"

"You worry too much about the impossible," Roderick said. "I've saved you. And now you are cursed by me to live. Let that be the end of it."

Edgar wanted to argue that he had earned the right to die.

He was starving, poor, devastated, a victim of constant tragedy, and worst of all he couldn't save his wife.

He wasn't even in love with his wife.

The one he loved was gone forever.

And the one he had always loved was a ghost on a beach. A memory in his mind. a dream that could never come true.

His real best friend had died years ago and the one he had now was a figment of his own twisted imagination.

"What kind of life have I had?" He asked Roderick. "Living in drunkenness and squalor. Marrying for convenience. Living in sin."

"Love isn't a sin," Roderick said, throwing Edgar's own words back at him. "That's what you told Petronella all those years ago, isn't it?"

"How do you know Petronella?"

"I know *you*," Roderick insisted. "Just as you know me. We are made of the same stuff, the same hearts, the same mad love that not everyone can bear. But don't give up on this world just yet, Edgar Allan Poe. You have so much greatness yet to achieve."

"I'm just a silly horror writer, Roderick," Edgar whispered, shaking his head. "The world doesn't need me."

Roderick gripped Edgar's shoulders and forced their eyes to meet.

"The world needs stories, Poe. And it needs yours.

Maybe they don't see it yet, maybe *you* don't see it yet—but you're changing the world."

Roderick vanished, and Edgar passed out.

He awoke again, later in the night in a pool of his own vomit, his hands sticky with the stuff. His fingers slick from going down his own throat.

He drank some water and went to sleep on the couch.

The next morning Virginia told him how wonderful she thought *The Raven* was; clearly believing it all to be a work of fiction.

Chapter 11

A million candles have burned themselves out. Still I read on.

Baltimore Maryland, 1847

The Poes returned home to Baltimore so that Virginia could live in peace until the end.

She had always loved this city.

With its smoky chimney skyline, and bay water-scented air.

And Poe loved her in the only way he could.

And this city was where they had first become family.

Where they had become friends.

Frances stopped coming round, unable to bear the sight of Virginia so sick. Edgar loathed her for it. If he had been permitted to sit by Petronella's side as she left this earth, he would've been there in a heartbeat. If he knew where Oscar was, and if Oscar were sick, Edgar would hold his hand until the end.

But not everyone had a heart as big as his.

One of the many maledictions of his life.

"Sit with me, Edgar," Virginia asked one night. "Tell me a story."

"You know all my stories, Sissy," he said, sitting on the edge of her bed.

Virginia smiled through the sickness plain in her cheeks.

"Tell me about Eleanora."

"What?"

"Tell me who it's really about. I know you claimed it was me and Oscar said it was that girl Elmira you loved in your youth, but I'm your wife and I can see when you're hiding the truth. So tell me who it's about. Tell me who all the love poems are about, Edgar."

"Virginia, you need to rest."

"Is it Annabel?"

"What?" Edgar said.

"You've said her name before. You called out to her once. When you were...unwell. Oscar and I didn't know who you meant. But she's one of the people you see, isn't she?"

Edgar held his wife's stare for a moment, her eyes burning bright despite the dimming of her skin.

"Yes," Edgar whispered.

"But I've never read about her," Virginia said. "I thought you only saw your characters."

"I thought so too."

"Tell me about her," Virginia breathed.

"Sissy—"

"Eddie," she cut in, "tell me your love story."

And so he did

Chapter 12

The Ballad of Edgar Allan Poe &
Annabel Lee

In a seaside village far away and in another time, a dark-haired girl named Annabel sat at the edge of the ocean eating a basket of strawberries as slowly as possible. It was a beautiful summer day and she was trying to make it last.

She finished the last strawberry far too soon.

She laid back in the sand, the sea-salt wind in her hair and the tangy beach air on her lips.

She smiled up into the sun.

She was supposed to be with her governess. Learning her Latin phrases for the day. Reading dreary books about the politics of the Kingdom. She did not care for it. It was tiresome and dull.

Beneath the strawberries in the basket she had stashed a book of ancient legends. She read them ravenously.

She never wanted to leave the beach on days like this.

The waves had begun to calm and the heat had reached an unbearable degree.

So Annabel shed her dress and dove into the water in only her shift—quite an unladylike sight.

She dove beneath wave after wave. She soon heard her mother calling to her from the top of the cliff that overlooked the beach. She ignored her and swam out just a bit further.

Just a bit.

One more wave.

Then she heard her mother scream.

The rush of water in her ears.

Then nothing.

* * *

On a cloudy November day, John Allan's belt buckle split open his foster son's lip, blood came gushing and spilling down his chin. Soon a small pool of evidence lay at Edgar's feet.

Edgar ran to his foster mother for comfort, but she was in bed again. She was always so fatigued. Always resting in her room with the lights off, the curtains closed, and the door locked.

She was always leaving Edgar alone with John Allan and his anger.

Edgar went to the lake down the lane from John Allan's plantation. The sky was full of storm clouds and Edgar's heart was full of desolation. He reached the lake, kicked off his shoes and waded into the water up to his knees.

It was bone chilling.

But it wasn't enough.

So he waded in up to his shoulders.

Then the sky opened up and began to cry.

And so did Edgar.

He was too young to have a soul that felt so aged. Weary from so much tragedy.

He sank beneath the water.

* * *

A few years after the year of her death Annabel was up in the highest tower of the castle reading a brand new book of legends when something in her heart told her to return to the beach.

She hadn't even tasted the salt of the ocean since the day she drowned.

In this place the sounds of the water were ever-present; the city overlooking the bluff.

"One day you will have to face your fears," her mentor had told her on a lonely, candlelit evening. "You cannot die a second time."

She knew that.

But she could feel the ache of life lost.

The disquiet of knowing what she'd left behind.

Cut down in her seventeenth year.

She could age here, in this place, if she wanted to. Plenty chose to grow old, then start all over again. But even as her mind matured and changed, she let her bones remain forever young.

She ignored the call of her favorite place in the world and condemned her heart to a lonely hell.

She punished herself for her childhood recklessness again and again no matter how many people in her death-life told her she shouldn't.

But on that fateful day she finally listened to the voice of the sea.

She followed the tug of the tides.

She reached the sandy shores right as a teenage boy washed up on the beach, coughing and sputtering.

He looked up at her and his entire life finally made sense.

Annabel walked over to him and offered him her hand.

"Hello," she said once he was standing before her. "I'm Annabel Lee."

"Hello, Annabel," the boy whispered around an ocean-coated tongue. "I'm Edgar Allan Poe."

"What are you doing here?" She asked, for she could see plain as day that he was very much alive.

"I was swimming."

She nodded. "So was I."

He looked at her dress—dry as a bone.

"Would you like to sit a while with me?" She asked. "I brought strawberries."

"Yes," Edgar said softly. "I think I would like that very much."

* * *

You know what happened next.

They fell madly in love.

Chapter 13

That the wind came out of the cloud by night, chilling and killing my Annabel Lee

Baltimore Maryland, still 1847

"That's such a beautiful love story," Virginia whispered. "Do you see her still?"

Edgar nodded as he squeezed Virginia's hand.

"Yes. Sometimes."

"On the beach?"

"On the beach."

"Do you think she is real?"

Edgar closed his eyes and tried to steady his breathing.

"She is real to me."

Virginia squeezed his hand back and he knew that she believed him.

"I'm tired, Edgar," Virginia whispered.

Edgar opened his eyes to realize he was crying profusely.

"Sissy," he whispered, leaning over Virginia, "please don't—" then he caught himself. He swallowed the words. He could not guilt her. Could not make her last moments in this world painful ones. He must make her feel at peace.

She was his friend.

She was his family.

"Virginia," he said, "it's okay. You can rest."

"Will you be okay, Eddie?"

No, he thought. *I will never be okay again.*

"I'll be alright, Sissy. It's okay, truly. You can go. You don't have to stay."

"I'm just so tired."

"I know," he whispered.

She gave him one last smile.

"Write about Annabel," she said.

"Sissy—"

"Promise me, Eddie."

"Alright. Alright. I promise."

"I love you, Edgar."

"I love you too, Virginia."

Then Mrs. Poe closed her eyes for good.

Edgar fell to the floor, his body racked by sobs.

It was said people out on the street could hear his cries late into the night.

ᛉ ᛉ ᛉ

Edgar watched as they lowered Virginia's casket into the ground.

Frances hadn't come.

"Edgar?"

He turned around to see Mary standing before him.

"Good God above," he breathed.

She gave him a weak smile.

"I worried I wouldn't get here in time. But when I heard I knew I had to come see you."

Edgar walked forward and fell into her arms.

But he ended up just crashing to the cemetery ground.

No one was there.

He was alone.

He looks amongst the tombstones. The words of the dead all around him. The voices of dozens of ghosts screaming in one horrible cacophony.

He wept like a child.

Then dragged himself to a pub and drank until he passed out and they had to call for him to be carried home.

He was the most famous he had ever been.

And the most alone.

Chapter 14

Neverwhere

Baltimore Maryland, 1849

For the first time in his life Edgar found his way to Roderick Usher's study without a panic attack and nightmarish hallucinations inciting him to do so.

"Usher," Edgar said and he entered. "It's been too long."

Roderick looked up from a book he was reading and almost smiled.

Edgar thought his mouth looked a bit odd trying to make a shape so foreign to him.

"Well, well, my good man, Poe. I started to think you'd forgotten about me."

Edgar sat down next to him by the fire.

"Never."

"That's good to hear."

Roderick poured him a glass of wine.

"Roderick, when I die, will you still go on?"

"Oh yes."

"Truly?"

"Poe, my story will go on for centuries."

* * *

When Edgar came back to his senses alone in his room, the images of Roderick and his wine completely dissipated; he set out to write.

And then an all too familiar rapping came at his window.

Poe steeled himself.

He gripped the edge of his desk and tried to will himself not to look.

But soon the incessant tapping of the creature's beak forced Edgar to settle his gaze upon the winged beast.

"What are you doing here?"

You called me.

"No," Edgar said, standing up, "I did not. I would never call you."

The bird made a sound Edgar could only describe as a laugh.

You are sick with loneliness, Poe.

"So what if I am?" Edgar countered. "There is nothing weak in feeling loneliness. It is natural. We all feel it. To lose those you love and fall into loneliness is normal. It is human."

What makes you think they ever loved you back?

"Stop," Edgar whispered. "They did."

Oscar left you. Virginia left you.

"She died! She did not choose to leave me."

The only constants in your life are your ghosts. Your hallucinations. Your madness is your only companion.

Edgar stood from his desk, picked up a book and threw it at the bird.

The bird vanished.

Edgar screamed.

* * *

"I think you've had enough to drink, Poe," the barkeep said.

Edgar's head lolled forward as the raven's voice dulled in his mind. The shadows that had followed him to the pub had slowly begun to melt away with every sip he took. Soon he found himself at the bottom of several pints of ale and his mind was wonderfully quiet.

Even his madness had finally left him.

Elmira.

Petronella.

His mother.

Henry.

Oscar.

Virginia.

Gone. Gone. Gone.

As he paid his tab he realized he didn't have any money left. Not for food or firewood. Nor paper and ink.

He was whispered about as he left the pub, stumbling out into the October air.

The famous Edgar Allan Poe.

Drunk on his feet without a penny to his name.

Or a single soul to call his companion.

Annabel, he thought forlornly.

She was a ghost.

Roderick wasn't a being of flesh and blood, but he had been a constant friend.

Edgar was so lonely.

It hurt.

Burned.

Ached.

He went to a corner store and purchased some whisky.

Stumbled his way down the street, drinking his fill.

"Poe," Roderick said, "stop, my friend. You're going too far."

Edgar stepped on Berenice's bloody teeth.

Nesace, Ligeia, Ianthe, and Angelo called out to him but he ignored them.

His own heart beat incessantly.

He ripped it out of his chest and left it on the sidewalk with his characters.

He smashed the now empty bottle against a wall.

And finally found his way to a lone bench right as his knees gave out.

He looked up at the stars.

"Edgar," Roderick said, sitting down next to him, "you must fight."

Edgar closed his eyes, fighting back decades of tears.

"I can't, Roderick. Not anymore. I just want to know peace for once in my pitiful existence."

"You are not pitiful."

Edgar opened his eyes and looked at his friend.

He looked so real.

He *was* real.

Real to him.

"Will you stay with me?" Edgar whispered.

Roderick reached out and took his hand.

"Until the end."

* * *

Days later Edgar awoke in a hospital bed, his head full of stars.

He looked to the corner of the room.

There were no shadows.

Only his characters.

All of them.

Not just the ones he'd come to know. But ones that had

never before haunted him. Arthur, and Lenore. Lenore and William. Auguste and Prince Prospero. Montressor and Fortunato. Camille and L'Espanaye. All the fairies and ghosts he ever penned into existence. The monsters that crawled forth from his quill; all stood before him, hands over their hearts.

"Thank you," Edgar whispered. "All of you."

Roderick stepped forward from the bunch, and placed his hand over Edgar's heart.

"I promise you Edgar," Roderick said, "the world will remember you. We will make sure of it."

Edgar nodded.

Looked at the ceiling and imagined the stars.

"Lord, help my poor soul."

Then the greatest poet who ever lived closed his eyes forevermore.

Chapter 15

And neither the angels in heaven above, nor the demons down under the sea, can ever dissever my soul from the soul of the beautiful Annabel Lee

After

Edgar rose from the water.

Annabel stood on the beach.

Looking as young as the day they met all those years ago.

Edgar held his own hands before his eyes. They were no longer the shaking, worn hands of a middle-aged man but the youthful, lean ones of his teenage self.

He felt lighter; the weariness he'd carried in his bones for so many years was finally gone.

The hollowness he'd harbored in his heart had finally lifted.

Annabel smiled and waded into the water to meet him.

"You're early," she said.

"I know," he replied, taking her hands in his. "I was impatient to meet you."

"That's alright," she said, pulling his hand to her mouth and kissing his chilled knuckles. "Your brother has been asking about you."

Edgar's heart leapt out of his chest and swam rapidly towards the shore.

"Henry's here?" He breathed.

Annabel smiled brighter.

"And Virginia. And Petronella. And your mother."

"How?" He whispered.

"Edgar, I thought you of all people would have figured it out by now."

Edgar just shook his head, terribly baffled and awestruck.

"This is the Kingdom of Heaven. Just beyond those cliffs."

Edgar felt tears of joy wet his cheeks.

"I...I get to go to Heaven?"

Annabel clutched his shaking hands tightly and stood on tiptoe to press her mouth to his. He wrapped his arms around her, pulling her as close to him as he could.

"Of course," she murmured against her mouth. "We've all been waiting so long. Come home, Edgar."

And he did.

Author's Note

I first discovered Edgar Allan Poe when I was twelve years old in Mr. Waggoner's 7th grade English class. We read *The Tell Tale Heart* and *The Raven* and I was immediately enamored. Poe quickly became my favorite poet and has since had an impact not just on my writing but on my life as a whole.

I've suffered with Major Depressive Disorder and suicidal ideations for years, so the way that Poe perfectly crafted into words how it felt to suffer from such immense sadness and loneliness was always something I connected with. I read his stories over and over throughout high school and college.

In 2019 I set out to make a documentary about him; The Hidden History of Edgar Allan Poe. It took me over a year to make. I traveled around Maryland and Delaware to film at The Deer Park Tavern, his grave, and his house in Baltimore. I interviewed authors, historians, actors, and Mr. Waggoner, about their opinions on his life and works, and more importantly how he had impacted their lives.

I obviously took creative liberties with Poe's life in this

story. The characters of Mary, Petronella, and Oscar are all creations from my imagination. As for Poe's bisexuality, that is something I dervived from numerous essays that analyzed *The Fall of the House of Usher* and *The Tell Tale Heart* through a queer lens. Plus someone heralded as being so strange and out of the ordinary by those he knew, it seems fitting to me that he might have been queer.

As for his wife Virginia, who we all know by now was alarmingly younger than him (and his cousin but that didn't really matter then and to this day cousin marriage is legal in the state of Maryland) historians differ in opinions on the nature of their relationship. Based on accounts of their friends at the time, and letters of his I've read in my years of research, I am a member of the team that believes they were just friends who married one another for convenience and protection. I changed the timeline of their marriage by several years in my story simply because even though by all means a marriage like theirs was accepted at the time, I am not above admitting how weird it would be now to read about a teenager marrying her adult cousin. I did not want to erase their marriage from this story, but I felt it was alright to tweak the timeline a bit.

I believe *Annabel Lee* was most likely about his childhood love, Elmira. But there is always that small chance she was actually an ethereal ghost he met during a suicide attempt when he was a teenager. Who's to say?

Lastly, I'd like to touch on his 'madness.' I discuss in my documentary that I believe—as many scholars, historians, and psychologists do—that Poe suffered from schizophrenia. Elements of this show up in many of his stories and poems, but seem the most evident in *The Fall of the House of Usher*. Roderick Usher is clearly (in my opinion) a personification of Poe's mental illness that it felt the most fitting for him to become the most prominent one of Poe's characters to keep reappearing throughout the story. I also believe the great 'mystery' around his death is just a way of invalidating his obvious struggles with mental illness. All signs point to accidental alcohol poisoning.

In the end I did indeed take many liberties with the history of Poe and his life and lots of places I just filled in the huge gaps of what we know with what I felt fit. I adore Poe. I am always in awe of his writing every time I pick up one of my (many) copies of his works for a reread.

I firmly believe Edgar Allan Poe was the greatest poet who ever lived and one of the most brilliant literary minds to ever grace our mortal realm. I hope wherever he is, he is finally at peace.

Acknowledgments

Many thanks to the following beautiful souls: My editor Katy Doyle. My best friend & cover artist Marcia Ruiz-Olguín. My mother. My 7th grade English teacher Mr. Waggoner. My followers, my hype team, my discord server folks. And of course the Master of the Macabre himself, Edgar Allan Poe. May he rest in peace.

About the Author

Molly Likovich is the author of *Riding The Headless Horseman,* its sequel *Getting With The Ghoul,* as well as titles such as *Send in The Clowns* and *There's Something in The Woods.* She is the co-author of *Not a Myth* and *The Willow's Silence.* She is also an accomplished poet with a BA in Creative Writing from Salisbury University. She can currently be found frolicking around the forest somewhere.

www.ingramcontent.com/pod-product-compliance
Lightning Source LLC
Chambersburg PA
CBHW031518010826
48973CB00013B/2715